BLATANT
LIES

Second Edition, 2023

ISBN: 9781658683524
ISBN-10: 1658683528
ISBN-13: 978-1658683524

Acknowledgments

Before we get started, I want to take a moment to sincerely thank *you*—the reader.

Seriously. Thank you!

This story is the result of a whole lot of input from so many individuals, even some who might never know it. I cheers to every single one of you.

I also offer kind appreciation to the editors of this book.

Please enjoy *Blatant Lies*.

Paul Knox

PAUL KNOX

BLATANT LIES

A REECE CANNON THRILLER

BLATANT LIES

A Reece Cannon Thriller: Volume 1

PAUL KNOX

Prologue

IS THIS WHAT I WANT ANYMORE?

Jessie Mistri sat alone by her kitchen window, watching a desert tree with thorny branches swaying to the light breeze. She wished the nearness of her partner felt like the wind's soft caress. Instead, her relationship hurt like those finger-length thorns, painful to touch or worse, to hold.

"I'll do what I want!" Dean had yelled, moments earlier, on his way out the front door before slamming it shut.

"I just want to start a family someday," Jessie had whispered after him. But he never heard it. He never heard anything she said, even if he were only a breath away.

I don't know what's happening to us—to me.

I have to do something.

*　*　*

Dean never came home that day.

Or ever again.

1

ONE YEAR LATER

HAWK KELLY PULLED a powdered, jelly donut from the box and took a big, cocky, messy bite. He stood at his boss's desk, listening to new intelligence at the secret CIA satellite facility in Tucson, Arizona.

"A mole?" Hawk asked, barely listening, with his mouth full and lips covered in white powder.

"I need you to dig in. Here's the file." Hawk's boss handed over a USB drive with the word *classified* etched on it. "And be serious about it. The intel that's been leaking is coming from this location. You'll find what you need in there."

"You...*nom-nom*, sure...*nom-nom*, about that?"

"Dammit, Hawk, wipe your face off. And read the files. Go!"

After exiting his boss's office, Hawk went back to his desk and casually perused through the material. Apparently the CIA didn't know exactly what was going on, but some overseas agents found a trail of information that shouldn't exist. The crumbs led back to the very same office where he worked.

Sticky jelly residue coated Hawk's powdered sugar-dusted computer keys. He didn't even notice, although his coworkers did.

Hawk was one of the best. Everybody knew that. He didn't have a lot to go on with this new lead, but finding valuable information when clues were scarce was second nature to him. That's why he was on this job. That's why he was on every important job.

He had connections.

As far as Hawk was concerned, the mole was as good as caught.

Nom-nom.

*   *   *

Reece Cannon drove her sheriff's SUV down an old-town road, scanning for anything that looked unusual or out of the ordinary. Anything at all. Although the new *Keeping-the-Peace-Since-1865* role she played for Pima County thrilled her imagination, nothing close to thrilling had actually happened.

She dreamed of solving uncrackable cases, ensnaring killers who fell into her traps, and rescuing the downtrodden. Lifting any and all to new heights, living their best life with inspired hope, she'd breathe free air into the lungs of her Tucsonans drowning in victimhood and despair.

"A fool's dream," she whispered as she drove alone.

Off the sides of the old road, the fingers of saguaro cacti reached for the heavens, and Reece imagined the shadows they cast held whispered secrets yet untold.

Before becoming a deputy, she worked the desk at a law firm, seeing struggle on victims' faces, hard knocks—what some call *real life*—and she wanted to be the difference between pain and hope, for others. Becoming a deputy was supposed to be her path to that goal.

Instead, she gave traffic tickets and labored over tedious paperwork about minor drug offenses and DUIs. Sure, it all needed to be done, but the glamorous and remarkably fulfilling fantasies were fading away.

The road Reece cruised down was weathered, with cracks snaking through the faded asphalt. Hardy creosote bushes and prickly pear cacti provided a splash of green here and there, with an occasional jackrabbit darting about, ears twitching with alertness, ever vigilant for the presence of predators.

Suddenly, a car whizzed by her, at least twenty over the forty-five MPH speed limit. Right next to her too, like the driver was oblivious to her official SUV. Either that or the individual simply didn't care.

"Cheers to another traffic ticket. Yay," Reece mumbled, flipping on her lights and speeding up, maneuvering behind the car.

After fifteen seconds of tailing the car that didn't slow, Reece prepared to switch her siren on. Before she could, the white Toyota Corolla quickly pulled off to the right, abruptly stopping.

Did you come from the bank with a stolen sack of gold coins?

Reece's ears perked up as she cranked her radio, hoping to hear an APB stating that a local bank had been robbed. A burglarized home? Lemonade stand?

No such luck. After a long, disappointing moment, she stepped out and cautiously approached the Corolla.

The window came down, and Reece found herself looking at a flustered young woman with puffy eyes and a wet face.

"I'm sorry, officer." *Sniff.* "I didn't know I was speeding." The woman tried to blink away her tears, but they just kept falling.

"Of course you didn't." Despite the show, Reece wasn't buying it.

"I didn't know what the speed limit was. It's my fiancé. I don't know what's going on." The woman looked up at Reece. "Wait, you're police, right?"

"I'm a sheriff's deputy."

"Oh. I must've driven farther than I thought." *Sniff.*

"I understand you're distraught, ma'am, but the speed limit is for everyone's protection. May I have your license and registration, please?"

"Mine?—oh…of course." The woman opened her purse and haphazardly fished around inside, unfocused, her long dark hair flying everywhere. She gushed, "Can I file a complaint?"

"Against me?"

"Oh, no, not against you. No, not at all. I think my fiancé's a…" Her breathing remained erratic as more tears fell down her face. "He's a… I'm…"

"Has someone hurt you, Ma'am?"

"No, it's not that"—*gasp, sniff*—"but I think he's a…a spy."

"A spy…" Reece took the driver's license from the woman and looked at her name. "…Ms. Mistri?"

The woman responded. "Ms. Mistri—for thirteen more days. Call me Jessie. You probably think I'm crazy. I would. I do. But I know the CIA well."

Jessie's breathing slightly calmed. She opened her glove box, pulling out papers. "My dad works for the CIA and so does Jack, my fiancé. I've grown up around it my entire life."

A hint of intrigue chipped at Reece's skepticism.

Jessie handed over her registration and insurance.

"Thank you. I'll be right back." Reece went to her SUV and searched the computer system for any additional info she could pull up on *Jessie Mistri*. There was a whole bunch of nothing, not even a single traffic ticket.

Back when Reece worked at the law firm, she'd heard cases too crazy to make up. *Truth is stranger than fiction*, as they say. Was it wrong to hope for a little excitement?

I can ask a few questions while she's stopped.

Reece returned to the Corolla. "So, Ms. Mistri, why not tell your father about this?" She handed the registration and insurance back to Jessie.

"My dad and Jack are practically best friends. If Jack is who I think he is—what is happening to me?— I can't believe I'm even saying this out loud." Jessie sniffed again but had a sliver of hope in her eyes as she stared up at Reece.

"If he is…foreign intelligence…I don't want my dad implicated somehow. He could be investigated. He's been in the CIA since before I was born. It's his life. And if Jack's not, I'm ruining my marriage that hasn't even begun yet."

"Your father would believe you, though, right?"

"He'd believe I *thought* I knew something. His job's all about getting in people's heads, and he thinks he knows everything. He'd support me, at least with words, but he'd tell Jack anyway. He'd give him a chance to explain. I've heard plenty of stories about all this before. When double agents have their cover blown, people die." Jessie winced. "I'm…" She shook her head, speechless.

"What makes you think your fiancé is foreign intelligence?"

"I heard him speaking in Farsi when he didn't know I was around."

"Farsi?"

"Jack's family heritage is Iranian. His last name is Darbandi. But Jack told me he never spoke or learned the language. As far as I knew, he only spoke English and then learned Mandarin in school."

"How do you know Farsi?"

"I've heard it before, from distant family members in India. I don't understand it, but they speak it there."

"Lying about knowing a language might be part of his job description, even to you. Could you be making this a bigger deal than it is? Why don't you talk to him about it?"

"I'm not!" Jessie wiped her eyes. "And something is off. He buys me flowers all the time and dotes on me and is too perfect."

"That doesn't exactly sound all that bad."

"But his…touch…is wrong. It's empty. I didn't realize it at first but now I can feel it. Nothing's there. It's like a big fake-out."

As Reece filled in a few more blanks on the ticket she was finishing, she started thinking relationship counseling seemed more appropriate than spy investigations.

Jessie continued. "Listen, my dad is a Deputy Executive Director. I don't know if you know, but that's a big deal. Jack is fairly new to the agency. He might be using me for the connection."

"That's quite the accusation." Trying to give her the benefit of the doubt, an idea came to Reece. "Any chance you could record a Farsi conversation of his? I'll check it out for you. If he's innocent, then no harm no foul, and nobody's the wiser for your suspicion. You can go back to living in peace. What do you think?" Reece finished writing the ticket and handed it over.

"Um…okay, I guess. Like a wiretap?"

"No, just download a recording app on your phone, turn the ringer off, and hide your phone. Does he have a home office?"

"Yes, that's where I heard him."

"Bingo. Hide it in his office. Record it and send me the file by email or Dropbox or something, if you want. Here's my contact info." Reece handed one of her cards over.

"Hopefully it's nothing. But until then…" Reece explained the traffic ticket and Jessie's options.

Back in her SUV, buckling her seatbelt, Reece tried to figure out if she'd just discovered espionage involving a foreign-intelligence fiancé, or simply gave a speeding ticket to a crazy lady.

Maybe it'd be a good joke for the water cooler.

Only time would tell.

2

JESSIE RETURNED TO THE ROAD, driving away from the sheriff's deputy. The ticket she'd just received was the least of her worries.

Glancing at the card she'd placed sideways in her center cup holder, she re-read, *Sheriff's Deputy Reece Cannon*. Could Jessie just be imagining everything at home? If so, she would gladly pay the speeding ticket, smile at traffic school, whatever it took.

She drove around aimlessly for a couple more hours, only stopping for a warm coffee from a Starbucks drive-through. The waterworks continued in unpredictable spurts. However, she did watch her speed a little more closely.

Though the Farsi-speaking lie of Jack's was the cause of her fears, it wasn't the cause of her tears. The sadness came because of what she recently came to realize about her and Jack's relationship.

Something was drastically wrong with the way Jack touched her. It was subtle. But as time wore on, the distance grew. The closer time marched towards the date of their wedding engagement, the further she felt from the man.

When she'd realized he'd lied to her, the emptiness she had tried to bury finally erupted.

He made dinners for her. But the conversations, superficial, waned. He kissed her. But his lips felt dull. He kept fresh flowers coming, one bouquet after another. But it was like a mission, like he had to, not a gift.

Jessie pulled into her driveway. Not that Jack would be home from work yet anyway, but upon opening the front door, she softly called out, "Jack?"

No answer. She stopped holding her breath.

Suddenly, out of nowhere, her furry companion Coco darted out from the hallway, wagging his tail with glee. She jumped, startled by the sudden movement. Letting out a sigh of relief, she felt grateful not to be alone after all.

How could she not think of Coco!? She honestly felt like all the stress was making her lose her mind.

She smiled at his joyful welcome. He leaped up and playfully jumped at her legs, pawing at her affectionately, licking her hands and nuzzling his nose against her.

Jessie pet him and scratched behind his ears. After a few moments she stood and took a deep breath. Now she had to record Jack's Farsi.

She searched the *Play Store* app on her Android. There were tons of recording apps that could do all sorts of things. She found one that was voice activated, meaning she could leave her phone hidden in his office and it would only start recording once he started talking. Perfect.

She hid the phone on the floor, wedged between the back of his desk and the wall. Little chance he'd discover it.

But now she didn't have a phone.

So she went to the bank, took out cash, bought a cheap phone with a fake name so Jack wouldn't find out, re-downloaded the app, and then hid her new phone in the spot she'd chosen.

Done for now.

Monday passed without Farsi, and Tuesday's sun began to set. She was now twelve, almost eleven, days away from being married to Jack Darbandi. Per usual, he'd been smiling and kissing her, but every touch made her feel like she was tumbling down a deeper and darker hole.

Perhaps she was just crazy. Maybe it wasn't even Farsi she had heard. Jack was probably just planning something secret for their wedding and Reece would tell her the amazing surprise.

Her own amateur spy efforts made her feel distant and twisted inside.

I need to do something to take my mind off this insanity.

Jessie decided to make a photo collage, a slideshow of friends, family, and the good times. Jessie would play the slideshow at her wedding as a thank you to everyone for being there.

After all, Jack professed to love her. Who in their right mind would ask for anything more than everything he'd already given her?

Now, where to get the pictures? Jessie went through her computer files and cloud storage. She found tons of pictures. The only problem was that she wasn't in a lot of them. She had been snapping the photos of others.

Then a thought occurred to her. What about her ex-boyfriend Dean's old photos? They'd dated for a few years, and he'd taken lots of pics of her and friends, usually at Jessie's request.

Did that runaway loser who left her still have his cloud storage? She remembered his old password.

Cringing at the thought of finding out that he deleted all the pictures of her, or worse, finding pictures of a new flame—she decided to do it anyway. Screw him.

She remembered he had slammed the door that day, after yet another fight they'd had, and then went off to his precious job at Hot Rods.

But he never returned. He skipped town and left her. He left everything.

Dean had said he loved cars, especially classic and fancy and expensive ones, but he left his job. Dean had said he loved Jessie, but he left her, too.

Stupid Dean Davis.

With one eye open, one eye closed, face turned half-sideways, Jessie opened Dean's storage. The password had been unchanged.

That's curious.

No new pictures. She opened her closed eye and prepared to dig into the material, starting at the end, thinking that he must've bought a new phone, started a new account, a new life.

Wait. What?

Jessie stared at the last picture taken in Dean's old cloud storage, the storage that had automatically backed up everything from his phone.

It was a picture of her fiancé's black Maserati, the one Jack drove now, the one he had always driven since Jessie met him shortly after Dean left. She knew it was Jack's because the license plate was the same.

Jack's Maserati was parked in the Hot Rods parking lot.

The sound of the front door opening snapped her out of it.

"Hey, baby, I'm home," called a familiar voice from the other room.

Jessie slammed her laptop closed as fast as she could, and jumped up, spinning around.

"Oh…hi," she stammered.

He moved closer to her.

Jessie felt her stomach twisting into knots as he hugged her, facing her desk. She felt Jack's chin on the back of her neck.

He was staring directly at the laptop.

3

MOLES WERE BAD.

Moles were especially bad for an agent like Hawk Kelly.

Not unsurprisingly, Hawk had a lead. He had sources, and one of the sources indicated that the mole might be Iranian. In fact, there was an extremely good chance of it.

The Tucson CIA office only had three to four dozen agents. Many of them posed as students at the University of Arizona, placed at the school to keep an eye on sensitive experiments and knowledge that had been funded by the government.

Assuming the Iranian mole looked or acted Iranian could be a mistake, but not entirely impossible. The Iranian or Iranian-descended agents at his facility only numbered two.

Hawk started his investigation with them.

Deputy Reece Cannon was sitting at her desk Wednesday morning when an email from Jessie came through. She hadn't recorded any Farsi conversations yet, but instead found an interesting picture she had sent over.

Her email detailed an ex-boyfriend of hers, Dean Davis, his love for classic cars, and his old job as a mechanic. He had worked at the Hot Rods classic car shop and restaurant in Old Vail, a sparsely populated area in Pima County that sat outside the southeastern edge of Tucson.

Unsuspectingly and oddly placed, at the end of its very own road, Hot Rods offered that old 1950s diner feel, complete with a unique view through a giant, dividing glass window in the center of the restaurant that overlooked a classic car shop, the other half of the business.

Jessie's ex-boyfriend allegedly disappeared one day and never came back. She thought he'd abandoned her after a bad fight and a failing relationship. Apparently, she'd never really questioned the fact that he'd also abandoned his old friends and his beloved job.

Bad times and bad blood may have led her to hasty assumptions.

Reece stared at the picture supposedly taken by this Dean-character the day he disappeared. It was an image of a sporty, expensive-looking Maserati that Jessie stated her fiancé owned.

Why did Dean take this picture, if he, in fact, had? Could Jack be involved in Dean's disappearance—and if so, why?

Reece took it upon herself to investigate. With no proof of anything having actually happened, she decided that alerting her superiors to the mysterious claims of a hysterical traffic-ticket recipient might be unwarranted.

She needed to get out on the road to do her beat, but could spare a few minutes to check this out. First stop, a little—actually, a lot—out of the way: Hot Rods.

A while later, she arrived.

The place smelled like burgers and fries, and looked like a throwback to her grandparents' day. A smiling waitress with an apron picked up a menu and greeted a fully uniformed Reece.

"Thanks, but I'm not here to eat." Reece looked around and saw another deputy, also a rookie, sitting alone in a booth, stuffing his face into a sloppy burger drenched in sauce.

His name: Ethan Wilson. A big guy, mostly muscle, he and his meal took the space for two. Maybe the face-stuffing meant he wouldn't notice her.

"Does your manager have an office?" Reece asked, slightly ducking her head in the opposite direction as Ethan. "I just have a couple questions about someone that used to work here."

"Sure, it's this way." Unfortunately, the waitress led Reece directly by Ethan's table. Right on her heels, Reece almost pushed the waitress forward, hoping he wouldn't see her.

Ethan looked up.

"Reece! Hey, what're you doing out here—I thought your beat was up in the Foothills?

"I'm not doing anything." Reece kept inching along even though the waitress had politely stopped.

"Are you here for the burgers? God, they're freakin' de-lish, and this sauce is bomb dot com. I'm hooked, I'm telling you!"

Wow.

"Ah, great. Didn't mean to interrupt." Reece hurried as fast as she could.

A minute later, Reece stood in a little office filled with boxes, talking with the manager.

"Dean? Of course I remember him. He worked here as a mechanic out in the shop"—the manager motioned towards the large window-wall that patrons could see the repair area through—"for years before no-call, no-showing one day. And never came back. I have no idea what happened to him, but he's missed. He was passionate about cars, and a genuine guy."

Reece looked out the giant window. There were a few mechanics working on an old, shiny, cream-colored classic car that was having something done to the engine. It looked very boutique.

"Can you look at a picture of a car for me—tell me if you recognize it?" Reece asked.

"Absolutely."

Reece pulled out a copy of the picture Jessie emailed, and handed it over.

"No, I don't recognize it. But that's our parking lot, obviously. Why?"

"Dean took this picture the last day he worked here. Any idea why he might've taken this picture?"

"Oh, yeah, that's also obvious."

"It is?"

"Sure, you see that Liberty Walk Rear Lip?" The manager pointed at the picture.

"The rear…the spoiler?" Reece asked.

"Yeah, the spoiler. It's custom and Dean would've loved that. A real enthusiast. He always talked about what he'd get if he were rich—actually, what he was *going* to get when he *got* rich. Showed me pics all the time. Classic, new, whatever. Shoot, I bet he could've fixed up a Pinto with enough customness and been sittin' pretty. Well, maybe not a Pinto, but he just loved cars. You get my drift, I'm sure."

"So if he saw this car out in the parking lot, he might've just gone out there and taken a picture of it?"

"Oh, hell yeah. No question. Probably did that at least once a week."

Reece thanked the manager. Then she left through a side door without Ethan getting a chance to see her again. He seemed like a good guy, but he never stopped talking about food, the gym, or bro stuff.

In her SUV, before driving away from Hot Rods, Reece wrote a quick email to Jessie asking if there were any more random car pictures Dean took, maybe even from the parking lot of Hot Rods.

Less than an hour later, she received a response, along with dozens of additional photos.

The manager was correct about Dean's picture-taking habit.

Dean took that picture.

And then he disappeared.

*   *   *

Jessie sat alone in her kitchen, the cold, smooth tile under her feet contrasting the warmth of her clammy skin. Jack would be home soon.

She felt caged in her own home. Why did it have to be like this? She needed to talk to someone, to let it all out. As she scrolled through her contacts, her thumb hovered over Maisie's name. Maisie was the kind of friend who would listen, even when the words were heavy and thorny.

Jessie hesitated for a moment, and then pressed *Call*. The phone rang once, twice, three times, each ring amplifying her anxiety. Then, as if a switch had been flipped, Maisie's voice filled her ear.

"Jessie, hey! What's going on?"

"Hey, Maisie. Look, I don't know where to start, but I need to talk. I think... I think Jack might be lying to me."

"Lying? About what?"

Jessie swallowed hard, the lump in her throat stubborn as a boulder. "I don't know, exactly. It's just a feeling. But, promise me you'll keep it to yourself, okay?"

"Of course, Jessie. I'm here for you. What's been going on? Did something happen?"

"Nothing specific. It's just…he's been acting strange lately. Listen, I don't really want to get into details." Jessie let out a sigh.

Maisie's tone grew serious. "Jessie, you're freaking me out. You know I'm here for you, right? Anything you need. I'm here."

Jessie felt the relief of Maisie's offer, like a hand extended in the darkness. "I know, Maisie. I really do."

"Let me help you. If you're worried, I can come over and we can talk it through."

"No, no. That's not necessary. I just…I needed to talk to someone, you know?"

"Okay, well, what about talking to a professional? I know a great therapist who could help."

Jessie shook her head, though Maisie couldn't see it. "I appreciate it, but I don't think that's what I need right now."

"Alright, but you have to promise me something. If things get worse, you need to let me know. I can call a lawyer or a detective or whatever you need. Or you can stay with me for a couple days."

"I will. I promise, Maisie. But I hope it doesn't come to that."

There was a pause, the silence between them holding unspoken tension. Finally, Maisie spoke. "Jessie, I'm just worried about you. You're like a sister to me, you know that, right?"

Jessie's voice cracked as she spoke, her emotions threatening to spill over. "I know, Maisie. You are too. Thank you. I feel better just talking to you."

"Good. Now, remember, I'm here for you, no matter what."

"I know. And I promise I'll keep you in the loop."

The call ended, and Jessie stared at her phone, the screen reflecting her worried face. She knew Maisie would be there for her, but for now, she didn't want to end up the crazy friend who needed attention for made-up stories or whatever. Just knowing her friend had her back made her feel stronger, the storm inside her a little less fierce.

Earlier that morning, Jessie had emailed the mysterious picture to Reece and then received a curious response from her asking for more pictures that Dean had taken. Maybe Reece believed, or at least, earnestly considered the story that Jessie feared true.

An only child, Jessie's mother had died during childbirth. Jessie's dad never paid her much attention, uninterested. He never even started a new family. Jack was the closest thing to a friend connection she'd ever seen him have.

There were few pictures of Jessie's childhood; she had taken care of herself. Her dad had loved her in the distracted way he knew how, and still did, but he remained too caught up in his CIA assignments and duties to, apparently, spend time with her. Overseeing departments and being integral to the agency, he always had an excuse.

And then Jessie, in essence, had dated her father: Dean Davis. Uninterested and devoted to his job, their relationship had been doomed to fail. She'd thought Dean just left her. And that seemed oddly normal.

That's why Jack seemed like such an angel. Jack's devotion to her broke the pattern, and Jessie was easily swept off her feet.

When Jessie first met Jack, he'd recently begun his career with the CIA. Jessie's dad was his superior, many ladder-rungs up. Jack's charm—disingenuous?—apparently also swept her dad off his feet, and Jessie's quick engagement to Jack followed.

Jack showed up soon after Dean left, and it all had seemed meant to be.

Maybe it *was* all meant to be.

Because maybe Jack meant it to be.

Jessie got up from the kitchen table and checked on her new, secret spy phone. The battery was almost dead. She recharged it and again placed it back in the hiding spot ready to record.

Soon she heard a key turning the lock in the front door. Jack was home.

I'm just crazy. This is all a mistake.

"Hi, I brought you flowers. I thought the other ones were looking droopy."

"Thanks, Jack. They're beautiful." Jessie busied herself, changing the vase's water and swapping the old bouquet for the new.

"Jack, can I ask you something?"

"Of course. Ask me anything."

"Do you like the burgers at Hot Rods?"

"The place your ex used to work at?"

"Uh-huh. I know we've never been, because, well, I hated the place, but I was just wondering if you wanted to go some time. We're getting married soon, and I've let bygones be bygones. *He's gone.*"

Jessie looked away, staring at the assortment of colorful carnations Jack had chosen this time.

"Sure. Whatever you want." Jack smiled, perfectly handsome. He even had cute dimples.

"You've never been?"

Jack leaned in and kissed her on the cheek.

"Nope."

4

A QUIET THURSDAY MORNING, Deputy Reece Cannon arrived to the station and went for some coffee. Moseying into the break room, she only found remnants of burnt stains at the bottom of the pot. After brewing a new batch, she happily filled a mug with the fresh, roasty goodness.

As she poured, footsteps sounded behind her.

"Is that you, Reece?" asked the strangely familiar voice.

Not possible. Could it really be?

Spinning around, her eyes matched the face to the voice.

"Tommy?—Tommy Shanahan!? What are you doing here?"

"Needed to talk to someone down here, and the smell of fresh coffee got me."

"No, I mean, you work here?"

"I do now—upstairs. I transferred last week from Picture Rocks. The drive was getting to me. Are you on a beat yet?" Shanahan asked.

"I've been doing my beat for about seven weeks now. You?"

"Been on the team for years, ever since high school. Recently made lieutenant." He grinned. "I have no idea why." Then: "Started working as a corrections officer while still going to the University."

"Congrats! But...you went to UofA? You could've gone to Harvard, or anywhere."

"I like it here. Still playing chess?"

"Not as much as I'd like." It was pure nostalgia, remembering the games they used to play. Back in school, Reece had been the chess champion of the entire state of Arizona.

As smart as he was, Shanahan had never won against Reece—but neither had anyone else.

Shanahan eyed the coffee pot. "Glad to see you around." He grabbed a mug from the cabinet.

"Not so fast, Shanahan. Maybe later we can catch up over a bite to eat or something. Unless, of course, you're busy learning another language tonight. How many do you speak now? Ten?"

He chuckled. "Currently, six. And it takes more than one night. Usually two." He winked.

Reece had missed Shanahan, the genius smartass two years older than her. He used to be a whiskey drinker too. Fun guy at a party.

"Anyway, I'm glad to bump into you." Reece changed the subject. "I have some interesting evidence that I think needs to be taken seriously. Maybe you can help me solve this one."

"'Interesting evidence' that needs solving? Isn't that above your pay grade, rookie?"

"But not above yours."

Shanahan quirked an eyebrow. "Please tell me you're not trying to get fired already."

Reece relayed the tale of Jessie's unlikely conundrum. Shanahan asked a couple questions and considered the story. Contemplating the unimaginable felt like old times again.

"Farsi, huh?" Shanahan asked.

"That's what she said."

"Get the recording and bring it to me. I'll translate. And pour me some of that coffee."

"Farsi's one of your six? And here I thought I'd have to use Google translate." Another person might've been surprised, but Reece wasn't just talking to a valedictorian, she was talking to, quite possibly, the most freakishly intelligent human being she'd ever met.

Shanahan held out his white mug with a quote on one side that read: *The secret of happiness is freedom, and the secret of freedom is courage. - Thucydides*

"Nice quote," Reece commented.

Shanahan glanced down at it. "Greek generals were badass and all, but I like this mug because it's jumbo sized. One can never have too much coffee. Anyway, don't you speak Spanish? Once you know one language, it's all the same."

Reece faintly grinned, tipping the coffee pot towards Thucydides' quote, pouring the warm liquid in his mug.

Shanahan smelled the steam rising and smiled. "You know, Farsi's not common in India, unless she's descended from the Parsis."

"How do you even know that?"

"Doesn't everybody?"

A few minutes later, Reece sat at her desk, firing up the computer and opening her email account.

One email in particular caught her attention.

5
EARLIER THAT MORNING

SOFT BLANKETS and a lovely pillow wrapped Jessie in comfy warmth as she awoke next to her fiancé Thursday morning. The new dawn traded fears for hope while dreamy visions still hung in the air.

Half asleep, she rolled over and put her arm around the man she wanted to be in love with.

No one was there.

Sitting up, she remembered. Everything. The clock read only 5:13 AM. She had stirred earlier than usual. Flinging herself out of bed, Jessie tiptoed into the main living room of her home, searching. Light shone from under the closed door of the converted bedroom—Jack's office.

She heard a language that her relatives from Mumbai had spoken when she'd visited India a couple years prior.

Farsi.

She stood there in the hallway, dressed in a pajama top and undies, listening, captivated. Suddenly Jack went silent, swiftly hanging up and opening the door.

Instantly half-closing her now extremely awake eyes, Jessie tried pretending to shuffle about, sleepily.

"Jessie. What are you doing?" Jack asked, unmoving. He wore his plaid gray and black robe as though he had risen from bed and immediately placed a call.

"Huh, me? Oh…looking for you, honeybuns. I…was lonely in bed without you." Jessie fought the fear rising like a cannon ball from her chest and into her throat. She tried her best to act normally, or maybe seductively, or basically any kind of act at all.

But Jessie was not good at acting or hiding her feelings—hence, the speeding-ticket breakdown in front of Deputy Reece Cannon. And Jessie knew it.

She went towards him and slid her hands over his shoulders and to his back, smashing her face against his chest so he couldn't analyze it.

"Oh. Did you need *something*? I guess I can spare a few minutes." Jack spoke as though he were a machine trying to imitate human emotion. He reciprocated Jessie's touch, moving his hands like a mirror's reflection of hers.

Jessie held her breath. There was no possible way she could pretend to be intimate with this man right now, no matter how much danger she was in.

"Why don't you take a shower and I'll meet you in bed?" she asked, still buried in his robe.

"I'll shower afterwards."

"For me?"

Jack didn't protest any further. His tone turned chipper. "Anything for you, my love." Dropping his arms, he pulled away, smiled at Jessie and headed for their master bathroom.

Jessie waited and listened. Soon she heard the shower water from the bathroom.

Did her secret phone get the recording? She needed to get it.

First, she went to their bedroom, peeking in like a stranger. The bathroom door was cracked open and hot steam drifted out. Jack was in there—at least for a minute or two.

And then she noticed his cell phone sitting on the nightstand.

Pausing for a moment, she thought of having been pressed against his plaid robe, which only had one single pocket in the front. She hadn't felt anything in it. And he had put both of his arms around her. Nothing had been in his hands.

Jack must've been talking Farsi on a secret phone that *he had*. And that phone must still be in his office somewhere.

She dashed back to his office and quickly searched through a few drawers but couldn't find any other phone.

It has to be here somewhere.

But there's no time.

Dropping to the floor, Jessie yanked her own secret phone from behind the desk and scurried out.

She needed to get out of the house.

Oh yeah, pants.

Rushing back into her bedroom, she reached for some jeans.

The white noise of the shower water stopped.

Jessie tugged the jeans on while hopping away.

The sound of the shower door opening echoed from inside the bathroom.

She had garden sandals by the front door. They would do. Sweeping up her small boho purse, she darted out of the house, closing the front door as quietly and quickly as possible.

Nineteen seconds later, Jessie sped down the neighborhood residential street in her white Toyota Corolla, trying to figure out what to tell Jack.

Jessie knew the spy game. She knew it way too well. And she believed that Dean hadn't just disappeared.

What would she say to Jack? Would he come after her?

*　*　*

Twenty minutes earlier, Jack Darbandi had already been staring at the bedroom ceiling for over a half-hour. He had an internal alarm clock that never failed. If anything, he awoke earlier than necessary, like today. His call was scheduled for 5:00 AM and he had every intention of taking it.

Being an Iranian intelligence officer took a life commitment, and his long-term goal of career advancement as a double agent seemed more promising than ever. Jessie's dad would, no doubt, pull some strings and get him up the food chain quicker than if he weren't married to his daughter.

Only the end goal mattered.

At 4:58 AM, Jack slid out of bed ever so gently, silently pulled on his robe and headed for his office. Having memorized every square inch of his American home, he didn't need lights.

His secret phone, designed to look just like an iPhone, stayed hidden under a removable tile in the floor of his office. It was the only physical piece of evidence connecting him to the Iranian government.

Holding the secret phone in his palms, the screen lit up. The call he expected came through.

"Jamshid, willing and able, sir," Jamshid 'Jack' Darbandi said, speaking in Farsi.

"All is well, Jamshid. The intelligence you have recently gathered and provided to us regarding Saudi Arabia has been extremely valuable. But we need more. We need to know what the Americans are planning to do about supporting Saudi's planned attacks against the Houthis in Yemen. We need specifics on weaponry and attack dates. Are you able to comply?"

"Absolutely, sir. My Deputy-Executive-Director contact will have access to that information and I will obtain pertinent details."

"Very well. Anything else to report, Jamshid?"

"Yes. I have recently discovered a classified document detailing the belief that there is information being leaked from my CIA facility out of Tucson. I'm not yet absolutely sure the document refers to my efforts and our home country, but caution is warranted."

"Find out and eliminate any threats." After a short pause, the man continued. "There's a possibility we will send two additional agents in the event they're needed."

"Yes, sir." Then: "May I ask who?"

"You are familiar with the Sasani brothers, correct?"

"Absolutely. Two of the best, sir."

"Expect a call from me at 5:00 AM, Saturday."

"Absolutely, sir, thank you. All loyalty to Iran." Jamshid/Jack quickly hung up, replaced the tile and opened his office door. An unexpected sight awaited him.

Jessie stood there, acting strange, shuffling her feet.

Listening?

What does she know?

"What are you doing?" he asked.

She called him "honeybuns" and approached him. He dutifully put his arms around her, wondering what the most appropriate course of action would be.

He wasn't sure if she was lonely, or rather, scrambling for an excuse to dodge suspicion. She might not have heard anything, but could he take that chance? Her dad had been enormously helpful in obtaining intelligence thus far, and Jack would hate to jeopardize that connection.

But jeopardize he would, without a second thought, if that meant securing his mission's integrity—especially if the Sasani brothers were coming. This was *his* mission, not theirs. He would complete it successfully and reap the glory.

He could not be found out.

For now, he would shower, plan, and pretend to love her. Depending on her actions over the next few hours, he would decide what needed to be done.

6

JESSIE HEADED for the closest Starbucks.

While standing in line with the early-morning crowd, Jessie created a new email account. Then she emailed the audio file she'd recorded to Deputy Reece Cannon, begging her to hurry.

While doing that, her phone rang. It was Jack.

"Baby, where'd you go?" he asked.

"I went to pick us up some post-*you know* coffees, as a thank you for everything you always do for me. It's still early. You don't have to leave for work for an hour or so, right?"

"Okay, well, hurry back." He paused. "I'm waiting."

Jessie tried to breathe. "Less than ten minutes, soon enough?" Her voice sounded detached, like someone else was talking at the end of a long tunnel.

"Perfect," Jack stated.

"I'm next, bye!" She tapped the red icon and waited. There were still two people ahead of her.

A few minutes later she sat in her car. What to do? Whatever she did, it needed to seem authentic. If Jack suspected anything, she might disappear like Dean had.

It took a few passing cars behind her, before she built up enough nerve.

A small gray pickup drove through the parking lot, and as soon as the cab passed, leaving the bed squarely in her rearview mirror, Jessie gunned it. The back of her Corolla slammed into the truck, harder than she expected, causing an accident right there in the parking lot of Starbucks at 5:32 AM.

The Corolla was nice and smashed in the back. It would definitely need to be towed, and that would take some time.

She felt intensely bad for the owner of the truck, but all in all, her insurance would pay for it and no one was hurt. The driver was fine—except for being irate at Jessie's supposed "blindness."

It was a lousy start to everyone's day, but on the bright side, there was plenty of coffee.

Thankfully, Jessie had her excuse for not going home.

And she hadn't disappeared—yet.

*   *   *

Dad is what she calls me.

I love that girl, even if I'm not good at showing it.

Jessie's dad, Prasan, was extremely grateful that his only daughter would soon be married to a real stand-up guy, someone he trusted, Jack Darbandi.

Thursday afternoon flew by for the Deputy Executive Director at the CIA, and the day was as typical as typical could be. He finished his work and planned on getting home for his new favorite show. His lazy cat waited for him, leftover bell pepper pasta with shrimp called his name, and the new Survivor would be available to stream tonight.

Life couldn't be better.

When the clock struck 5:00 PM, he snapped shut his briefcase, and left the office.

A little later, in the middle of savoring his delicious pasta, there was a knock at the door. He grunted, stood up and answered. To his surprise, Jack stood there smiling.

"Jacky boy, I didn't expect you over tonight. Come in. What's going on?"

"What's that smell, Prasan?"

"That's the smell of red bell-pepper goodness— with shrimp! I have a giant tub of it. Here, let me make you a plate." He turned and headed to the kitchen.

"Have you talked to Jessie today?" Jack asked.

"No," Prasan called out, still walking. "She's not getting cold feet, is she?"

Prasan turned around, expecting an answer, but found that his future son-in-law had a weapon pointed at him.

The burn of a single bullet piercing his heart was the last thing Jessie's dad ever felt.

*   *   *

Jack Darbandi shot a bullet straight through Jessie's dad's chest with the utmost precision, fired from a suppressor-equipped Glock 9mm. Then he shot the dead man a couple more times in random locations.

Instead of disposing of the body and tidying up, Jack made the house look like a wreck, knocking over living room furniture like an amateur burglar had broken in before Prasan got home, a fight had ensued, and then the burglar unwillingly shot at the old man.

Then, Jack ate the rest of the pasta and washed the plate.

He knew the bullets couldn't be traced to his unregistered gun, no fingerprints would be found, he wouldn't be discovered, and it wouldn't look like an Iranian spy needed the CIA Deputy Executive Director out of the way.

Just as Jack calmly opened the front door to leave, about to remove his gloves, the dead man's phone rang.

Who could that be?

Shutting the door, he walked over to the body, pulled the CIA-issued cell phone from his pocket and checked who the caller might be. Not in the contact list, the number simply showed up as ten digits.

Jack took out his personal phone and googled the number. A result pulled right up—the Pima County Sheriff's Department.

Highly unlikely this is regarding Jessie's car accident. But even if she told the PCSD something about hearing me speak Farsi, are they even smart enough to suspect something?

He slipped the phone back in Prasan's pocket, annoyed at the additional complications.

Then he left, driving off in his Maserati and thinking about his next move.

Questions needed answers.

He headed home.

7

EARLIER THAT THURSDAY MORNING, at 9:18 AM, Reece sipped her fresh mug of coffee, still smiling from seeing Tommy Shanahan again. When she opened her emails, interestingly, there was one from Jessie with an audio attachment, sent almost four hours earlier.

Reece opened it, listened, and although it was slightly muffled, she heard a man speaking a foreign language she was unfamiliar with.

Finding Lieutenant Shanahan didn't take long, but when she did, he was busy collaborating with one of his subordinates, a deputy in the Violent Crimes Section about a string of robberies. Reece's recording had to wait its turn.

A little while later, reluctantly, she had to leave for her beat. All day she waited for a call from Shanahan, but to her dismay, a call never came.

That afternoon, while still out, Reece received another email from Jessie, asking if she'd translated it yet. Reece could only reply: *Not yet. I'll be in touch ASAP.*

As Reece's day neared the end, her routes completed, she headed back to the station. Upon entering, she went straight to Shanahan's desk, smelling an aroma of peppermint breath mints wafting and clouding around his head.

He was translating the recording.

Finally!

Shanahan looked up with a grave expression as she approached. "This guy's Iranian intelligence. That is, if this recording isn't a hoax."

Reece said, "If it's a joke or something, that woman deserves an award for actress of the year. There's no way. What did he say—and what took you so long?"

"Been a long day. Crime doesn't stop because other crime calls." Shanahan recounted what Jack had said, including the bit about the CIA "Deputy-Executive-Director contact" and "loyalty to Iran."

"So he's dirty." Reece squinted.

"He's all bad. The proof is right here—kind of. An audio recording like this might be enough for the CIA to investigate internally, but I can't get an arrest warrant without some kind of definitive proof of wrongdoing. However, if this is real, Reece, this is serious. We need to alert Chief Gomez so he can contact the CIA. This is out—way out—of our hands."

Chief Gomez was one of the nicest people Reece had met here so far. Big and round, his belly shook like a bowl of Jell-O and he laughed like Santa Clause. He was also Lieutenant Shanahan's superior.

Reece followed Shanahan to Chief Gomez's office, but they discovered the Chief had already gone home for the day. Shanahan dialed Gomez's cell. It went straight to voicemail.

After hanging up, Shanahan relayed: "His recording says he left for vacation, out fishing and camping and won't have service. Let's go talk to Sheriff Landy."

Then the pair went to Gomez's boss, the boss of all bosses at the station, Sheriff Luke Landy himself.

However, Sheriff Landy was also gone for the day, and Shanahan then called his personal phone too. Another voicemail.

After leaving a message, Shanahan said, "Landy isn't on vacation, thankfully, but he's known to never call back unless he's on the clock. Being *so important* means you don't have to deal with the little stuff. He'll be here tomorrow, though."

"Iranian espionage?" Reece monotoned.

"He's not going to call back. The place could burn down and he'd show up tomorrow acting like he never knew. I don't know what's up with that guy, but he plays the bureaucrat card well. He's lucky to keep getting elected, that's all I can say."

"Who next?" Reece asked.

"We call the CIA."

"I hope Jessie's wrong." Reece explained to Shanahan about Jessie's father and the implications Jessie hoped to avoid.

"Some things are too important, Reece. This isn't coming down on me. But—if Jessie's dad is a decision maker over there, then he might be a good person to contact first. He could decide what to do about this alleged double agent, or how to report him. Also, if Jessie's dad puts the brakes on this guy, then how incriminating could that be for him? Won't he be the hero?"

"Okay, fair enough. You're right. Let's call him."

"What's his number?"

"Jessie's last name is Mistri. Can we look up a Deputy Executive Director with that last name?"

"I can do it." Shanahan went back to his desk and Reece followed. It didn't take more than fifteen minutes, a couple calls, Shanahan's credentials and reason for calling, and they had Prasan Mistri's work cell. Reece checked the time. It was a quarter to 6:00 PM.

To their dismay, it rang and rang until they received a third voicemail.

Reece fought back her frustration. "Let's give the man a little time to finish dinner and call us back. He's CIA, we're the law, and this is espionage. I'm *sure* he'll call us back…soon." At this point, Reece only *hoped* more than she was sure.

Shanahan sat back in his chair for a moment, thinking. "Very well. We'll wait for a few minutes. Since I'm bereft of options anyway, and dinner sounds pretty good, I'm headed home. I'll let you know as soon as he calls me back."

Shanahan took out a small container from his pocket and dropped two breath mints into his hand, tossing them back.

"What's with the peppermints?" Reece asked.

"Mint improves brain function. It's scientifically proven." And with that, Shanahan popped up from his chair and strode off.

With nothing else to do but wait, Reece also went home.

On her way, she phoned Jessie.

One short, half-ring later, an anxious voice answered. "Hello—Deputy Cannon?"

"Ms. Mistri, yes, this is she."

"Please, call me Jessie. Could you translate it?"

"Someone else here, Lieutenant Tommy Shanahan, did. He speaks Farsi. I'm afraid you might be right. By the sound of the recording, Jack appears to be an Iranian informant of some kind."

Silence.

"Are you there, Ms… Jessie?"

"Yes, yes, sorry." The sound of a strained voice, thick with emotion, cracked. "I don't know what to do."

What would Reece advise if she were the one making decisions? Actually, she *was* the one making decisions. Nobody else was around.

Reece asked, "Can you get his phone—the one he spoke Farsi on? It might help my investigation."

"I...I...Okay. He's still at work. It has to be in his office somewhere. I'll look. I can't leave anyway, my car's wrecked."

"You wrecked your car?"

"Yeah."

"You didn't slow down, especially crying like that?"

"It wasn't that. I needed an alibi for...it's a long story."

"Jack?"

"Yeah. Jack."

"Get the phone and call me. I'll pick you up myself. And if you feel in danger for any reason, call me immediately."

*   *   *

Jamshid "Jack" Darbandi stormed inside his home looking for Jessie, but she was nowhere to be found. He still wasn't completely sure she even knew or suspected anything, but nothing could be risked.

Jamshid had believed Prasan when he'd said he hadn't talked with her. As long as Jessie hadn't told the sheriff's department anything, the CIA also didn't know his true colors.

But why did the PCSD call?

Aborting the mission would bring him shame. He couldn't have that.

Walking straight to his office, he removed the secret tile and drew out his phone, punching in the password and dialing his Iranian contacts.

Five rings later, a superior from his agency picked up. "Jamshid? What is the meaning of this?"

"Sir, the mission may have been compromised. But only temporarily. I can fix it. My marriage to Jessie will not go through as planned. She *may* have overheard our previous conversation. I have eliminated her father, and next, will eliminate her as well. First, I must interrogate her to find out if she has spoken to anyone else about this. I don't think she has, or if she even knows anything, but I risk nothing. My allegiance is to Iran at all costs."

"That is disappointing, Jamshid. Highly disappointing. Especially because we need you to verify recent intelligence suggesting a covert Saudi operative is posing as an agent in your CIA office. Eliminate any and all possible threats to this mission. And find the Saudi operative. Remember, you are not important, either. You will be disavowed if discovered.

And you know what to do in that scenario. Are we clear?"

"Of course. I will call when finished." Jamshid hung up and threw the phone back under the tile. The mere thought of being disavowed filled him with rage. He'd be damned before taking the poison pill because of Jessie. That would never happen. Never.

He called her friend Maisie, and then a couple more of her main girlfriends, but none of them had heard from her—or at least that's what they said.

His fiancé couldn't have gone far on foot.

*   *   *

Jessie hadn't gone far at all. Hiding in the shallow bedroom closet, having barely slid shut the closet door before he had rushed in, she listened to the entire conversation.

Having been looking for the phone in silence, she had heard Jack open the front door. With nowhere to go except the closet, she jumped inside. Huddled behind the door, she had prayed, sweat, and shook. Yet she remained unknown.

Not speaking Farsi, she didn't know what he'd said, but by the tone of his voice, it didn't sound happy. And he said *her name*.

But now she knew where the phone was hidden.

As soon as Jack left, presumably to search for her, she removed the loose tile, lifted the phone like a bone from a tomb, and then called Deputy Reece Cannon.

"I'll be right there," Reece said.

"Hurry!" Jessie pleaded.

Now Jessie could only wait, shaking and trembling and looking a mess, for the only person she was willing to rely on right now.

Please don't come home, please don't come home, please don't...

8

REECE HAD ANSWERED Jessie's call immediately. News from Shanahan speaking to someone would've been good, but finding the phone was even better. It invigorated the rookie. Reece had imagined living for these moments—but she needed Jessie to actually remain living, too.

After hanging up with the woman, Reece dialed Shanahan. "Jessie has the phone. I'm on my way to pick her up right now."

"What? Okay. Wow. I'm still waiting on Prasan to call me back, but this is getting seriouser and seriouser."

"Curiouser and curiouser?" Reece felt a little like Alice.

"I'll leave that up to the CIA. I'm calling them directly. We need to get this in the right hands."

"Do it." Reece hung up and drove as fast as she could, berries and cherries flashing. A block from Jessie's house, she shut them off.

Reece wasn't qualified for this and she knew it. It still felt great, though. She'd do what she could.

Lieutenant Shanahan hung up with Reece and twisted the cap back on the bottle, wishing he hadn't just taken that shot o' whiskey.

The corned beef leftovers currently reheating in the microwave would have to wait.

Once again, he dialed the CIA.

After being routed up the chain of command, he spoke with a cautious-sounding director who promised him a call back ASAP.

Waiting for what felt like the hundredth call back, Shanahan eyed his bottle.

Actually, he silently rationalized, he'd barely even begun drinking for the night. He didn't even feel it. What was one more shot?

Reece had pulled her sheriff's SUV into a gas station parking lot around the corner from Jessie's neighborhood, staring at the odd iPhone lookalike while Jessie sat passenger. It was password protected.

"Do you think we should try to unlock it?" Jessie asked.

"Probably not," Reece muttered, thinking of something very peculiar.

Shanahan had said they needed evidence for an arrest. Maybe the phone would be good enough.

Maybe all of this will end up in the CIA's hands, but...

If she knew the phone's number, Shanahan could call, speak Farsi to Jack, pretend to be an Iranian operative and ask questions about the whereabouts of Dean or his body. Whether they found a body or not, they could record the confession and have all the evidence they needed for a good ol' fashioned arrest.

Quite possibly irresponsible, maybe futile, but perhaps brilliant?

Only a rookie would try it. But was she being naïve? She pushed that thought from her mind.

The password. She wanted it. Would Shanahan agree to this?

"Do you know any of Jack's passwords?"

"I know one he uses for little stuff." Jessie recited the password and Reece punched it in.

The screen shook. Words appeared: *Two attempts remaining.*

"I need to get this right or we get locked out—or worse," Reece said. "I know someone to call."

Once again, Reece called Shanahan, telling him the outlandish, makeshift plan she'd concocted and the password dilemma.

"That sounds absolutely ludicrous, Reece."

"Does anyone even care yet? Or is everyone busy eating dinner still?"

"I'm not getting anywhere with the CIA. Still waiting for a call back. And Jessie's dad isn't calling back either."

"There's a foreign spy, possibly a killer, who we potentially need off the streets—right now. Don't you think?" Reece pressed.

"Landy didn't call back either, per usual," Shanahan muttered.

Then he chuckled. "I hope Gomez is catching something good right now because he's gonna need one hell of a whopper to beat this story around the water cooler—*if* we get the number."

"So you're in?"

"Let's get the number. But that's it," Shanahan answered.

"We need the password, first, *genius*." Reece waited.

"Any hints on the home screen?" he asked.

"Nope. Could be anything."

"I doubt it could be *anything*. Let me think for a second. Is it just numbers and letters?"

Reece looked at the screen. "No. Looks like you can input numbers, letters and a few other characters."

"What other characters?"

"Normal stuff, like parentheses, plus and minus signs, and even those carrot top-looking things."

"The password might be an equation. Otherwise there would be no need for those symbols. Do you think there's the possibility he's had this phone for years, before facial recognition?"

Reece looked at Jessie. "How long has Jack been in the country?"

"He was born here, as far as I or anyone knew. His parents supposedly died in a car crash when he was young."

"Well, that's probably all been faked." Reece turned her attention back to the phone. "Yeah, he's been here a while. This phone, on the outside, looks like an old iPhone, thick and small, like maybe third or fourth generation if I remember right."

"Was Jack into math at all? Any equations he's particularly fond of?"

"Who's particularly fond of math equations except you?"

"Just ask Jessie."

Jessie spoke. "I heard him. No, he didn't talk math. Well, actually, there was one time he commented on the achievements of Maryam Mir—something—a famous Iranian—who was on the news one time. I think she was a mathematician."

"How do you remember that?" Reece asked.

"I have a good memory—always have. I don't drink."

"She says something about Maryam—"

"I heard her. And I'm thinking. And tell her that there're plenty of people who drink that have good memories."

"Uh, I don't know if now is the time—"

"I heard him," Jessie responded. "Tell him that *drinking* clouds the mind. Sober people remember stuff better."

"Can you tell her to just be quiet for a second?" snapped Shanahan.

Reece scrunched up her face. Was she really playing telephone with these two people right now?

Shanahan then announced, "Try this: lowercase c, capital L, carrot symbol, open parenthesis, the number six, lowercase g, the minus sign, the number six, and the close parenthesis. It's a long shot, probably won't work, but it might be worth a try."

"What the…sure, okay." Reece inputted *cL^(6g-6)* into the phone.

It worked.

The phone unlocked.

"How the hell did you know that? It worked! First try. Holy mother, I'll never doubt you again, Shanahan."

"You doubted me?"

"No, I suppose…no."

Shanahan sounded merry. "I just tried Maryam's famous equation stating that the number of simple closed geodesics of length less than L, is polynomial in L—"

Reece interrupted. "I'll call you back. Let me find this device's number."

"Maryam Mirzakhani was a brilliant Iranian mathematician. It was a no-brainer. Bye." And with that, the amateur whiskey-drinking mathematician, Tommy Shanahan, again hung up.

It didn't take long. Reece found the phone's own number. She typed it in her cell's contact list and also texted it to Shanahan.

Then she began heading back to Jessie's house. Reece explained the new plan on the way.

"You want me to put the phone *back*?" A look of terror erupted across Jessie's face.

"I'll wait here and cover you the entire time."

"I thought you wanted the phone."

"I want his ass behind bars even more."

"You swear you'll stop him if he comes back?"

"You bet. Just hurry—we're talking thirty seconds or less, right?" Reece parked. There was still no car in Jessie's driveway, no sign that Jack was there.

"Thirty seconds." Jessie jumped out, ran inside, and in less than a minute was again a passenger in Reece's SUV.

"You got the phone back where you found it?" Reece asked.

"Yes."

Reece headed home.

9

LIEUTENANT TOMMY SHANAHAN hung up with Reece, the rookie, the old friend. He smirked. It was nice putting his skills to work. Maybe he'd even have another opportunity to do that before this was all said and done.

Wait a sec. If this plan of hers works, that means the phone has to go back. Oh, shit.

Just then his phone rang. It was the CIA.

"Is this Lieutenant Shanahan?" the voice asked.

"Yes, sir. May I ask who this is?"

"This is me," the voice answered.

Shanahan rolled his eyes. "This is Lieutenant Tommy Shanahan with the Pima County Sheriff's Department. I have information about the possibility of an Iranian intelligence operative. I'm going to need a name and an official title for my report."

"There's not going to be a report. But you can call me Hawk. My title is Boss. I don't even exist, anyway, and this isn't officially happening."

"Okay, Hawk, we have—"

"Let me stop you, buddy. I already know what you've relayed thus far. Anything new since then?"

"No." Shanahan wasn't about to divulge what he and Reece just did. The plan sounded more and more stupid the longer he thought about it. Almost as stupid as this Hawk-guy sounded.

"So, you have his phone, like, the contact phone for the Iranian government?" Hawk asked.

"We might."

"You might or you do?"

Shanahan cringed. "We do."

"Alright, listen, I don't want another word of this spoken to anyone. This is top-secret, above your pay grade, classified. I don't even want to be discussing this over the phone anymore. Do I make myself clear?"

"Absolutely, sir. Should I stand by for proper procedure?"

"No. You're done with this. I don't want any paperwork, nothing. Pima County doesn't even know this ever happened."

Shanahan picked up his whiskey bottle. "Right."

"Does anyone else know about this?" Hawk asked.

Shanahan ran his fingers around the cap. "Deputy Reece Cannon is in contact with the suspect's fiancée, Jessie Mistri."

Hawk asked for Reece's number and Shanahan gave it to him, along with the assurance Jessie would be safe with her.

Hawk continued. "Send Jessie back to her house with the phone. Put the phone back. Tell Jessie to stay there, acting normal. I'll be there in a few minutes to handle the situation."

Shanahan set the bottle down. "Sure, I'll get the phone put back. No problem."

But his relief quickly faded. "Are you sure we should leave an innocent civilian in harm's way?"

"Lieutenant, do as you're told."

Hawk disconnected, and Shanahan stared at his phone in disbelief.

An incoming text message chimed. It was Reece. She had the number.

Shanahan didn't like being told what to do, at least not like *that*. Putting a civilian at risk was inexcusable. If something were to happen to her...

Nothing is going to happen to her. I'll make sure of that.

Shanahan requested an Uber. He used them all the time. It was almost second nature, his normal way of getting around when he wasn't on the clock.

Then he picked up his bottle and took one last, long, tasty swig.

The Uber was nearby. Two minutes later, Shanahan headed to Jessie's house with his badge out and a temporary mount-grill light flashing on the top of the vehicle.

"Don't worry about any tickets—you're an honorary deputy," he assured the young driver.

Thankfully, the driver was not only fine with the excitement, but seemed thrilled to be able to play cop for a minute.

Shanahan didn't care if it was against policy or not. Hell, this wasn't even "officially happening."

Then he placed a call to Reece.

*   *   *

"There's no way I'm leaving her there. The agent really said that? That doesn't even make sense." Reece flipped her SUV around and headed back to Jessie's house with the full intention of staying until this mysterious Hawk-person showed up.

"Don't worry, I'm on my way. I'll watch the house."

"Oh, is dinner over?"

"Damn. I left it in the microwave. You owe me some corned beef."

"I'll even bring the cabbage. Listen, if you're on the way, I'm going to Prasan's house to personally tell him what's going on. None of this sounds right."

Jessie piped up. "My dad? And an agent is on the way to my house? I thought—"

"This is too big," Reece interrupted. "We tried your dad, first, but he's not calling us back. I'll go tell him myself."

"You called my dad!?" Jessie asked in disbelief. "I thought I could trust you."

"You *can* trust me—with your life." Reece addressed Shanahan. "How far are you?"

"A couple minutes, max. You?"

"I'm already back." Reece looked at Jessie. "What's your dad's address?"

"Is he there?" Shanahan asked.

"No. Wait, who?" Reece asked.

"Anyone," Shanahan said.

Jessie recited her dad's address to Reece.

"No, no one's here," Reece answered. "I'm leaving ASAP. It doesn't smell right to me."

"You're a rookie, Reece. Nothing smells right to you. But go. I'm ninety seconds away."

Jessie reluctantly exited the SUV, but then hurried up her driveway until she made it through the front door, unharmed, alone. Before she shut the door, she turned and gave Reece a long, melancholy stare.

Reece met her gaze and nodded. *I'm not leaving you alone.*

Jessie closed the door.

"You here?" Reece asked Shanahan.

"Pulling up now."

"What the…what are you in?" Reece watched as a little blue RAV4 pulled up with a mount grill atop, flashing like a joke, and two stickers on the back that read *Uber* and *Lyft*.

"Long story. I'll be here. Go tell her dad," he said, as Reece watched Lieutenant Shanahan exit the RAV4.

Reece sped off, wondering the full extent of shenanigans this night would bring.

* * *

Jessie closed the front door and went into the kitchen. Wait, where was Coco to greet her?

The house was cold, like the AC had been set too low. She flipped on the kitchen spotlighting, hot little halogen bulbs that added a warm yellow glow to the wood cabinetry.

A voice startled her.

"Sit down, dear. I think we have something to talk about."

Jack emerged from the shadows with Coco in his arms, methodically petting his head. "And do be quiet. I would hate to hurt your pretty face, or the dim-witted deputy that thinks he's watching the place."

Jessie wouldn't have been able to make a peep anyway. To her credit, she tried, but no sound escaped. She was much too frightened, frozen in place, staring.

Next to Jack, on the counter, sat a large role of gray duct tape. And a gun.

Jack reached for the gun, placing his finger on the trigger, and then motioned for her to sit at the kitchen table.

"Shhh," he breathed out.

10

HAWK KELLY hung up with Lieutenant Shanahan and tossed his phone beside him on the couch.

He'd been home for the night, flipping through all the shows he'd already watched on Netflix, thinking about the Iranian case and what that meant for Saudi Arabia, when he received the call about a lieutenant at the sheriff's department with information.

After talking to Shanahan, he planned on calling Reece next, but first grabbed a chicken drumstick from the KFC bucket and gnawed on it, spilling some of the oily breading on his shirt, probably staining it. Eh.

He picked up his phone again, sighed, and let his greasy fingers slip and slide over the keys until he had Reece on the other end.

"Forget the case," he'd also told her. "No reports, no nothing," he reiterated.

"Okay," was all that she'd said in response. She didn't even care who he was, how *important* he was.

Great. Her insolence was good for him. Another American who didn't give a rat's ass about anything. He stuffed another large bite of fried meat into his mouth and ground his teeth before getting up to leave for Jessie's house.

He'd get there. He'd deal with Jack, or Jamshid, or whoever he was. And he'd deal with Jessie too.

Hawk chuckled at the stupid deputies, almost choking on his chicken.

Americans. They're all so pitiful. But their food is to die for.

*   *   *

Deputy Reece Cannon arrived at Prasan's house about ten minutes later. Almost 9:00 PM, traffic was light. Jessie and her dad both lived on the North side of Tucson, in a beautiful area called the Catalina Foothills.

Prasan's home was somewhat secluded, tucked away on an acre or two of land with desert shrubbery surrounding a spacious-looking home. A car sat in the circular driveway and lights were on inside.

Finding him seemed promising.

After a few rounds of knocks, impatient foot-tapping amidst the sound of crickets chirping, and more knocks without any answer or response, Reece couldn't wait any longer. Still in uniform, she decided to peek through a window around the side of the home.

When she looked inside, she gasped.

Reece tried the front door—unlocked. She tore in, found a destroyed home and corpse with bloody holes through his chest. She immediately called for backup and CSI.

Unable to shake the feeling that Hawk's request had been out of line, Reece only wanted to get back to Jessie's house, to keep her safe.

Maybe everything will be fine over there and Hawk will get Jessie to safety.

Or maybe not.

Shanahan might need backup.

Reece didn't wait for CSI. There was nothing she could do there anyway.

She raced back to Jessie's house. On the way there she called Shanahan, telling him that she headed his way.

He answered, but she heard something on the other end, in the background, and it sounded terribly, terribly wrong.

11

THE DUCT TAPE around Jessie's wrists gave her no choice but to sit still. With red-rimmed eyes, a tearstained face, her fiancé pointing an efficient-looking gun at her—not to mention Reece having left her—it was safe to say that Jessie's hopes and dreams were forgotten and the tape that bound her to the chair clung to one last desire: staying alive.

She had no reason to lie. If anything, the truth might keep her breathing for a moment longer. Well, maybe not the *entire* truth.

"So you've been in contact with this Deputy Reece Cannon and told her you think I'm a double agent? What?—you didn't like the carnations? I thought they were lovely."

"Are you even capable of love? You killed Dean! Didn't you!?"

"If it makes you feel any better, it was quick. And if you close your eyes, it will be for you too. And yes, I loved you. Or at least, what being with you did for me. It's too bad that's over. I could've had it so good."

Jessie half-coughed, half-whimpered, wondering if she had enough tears streaming down her face to wet the duct tape around her hands and loosen it.

Jack continued. "But I might let you live if you tell me why that idiot out there is even out there. Maybe if you tell me the truth, I'll just go back to Iran and forget it...and forget all about you. But I need the whole truth from you, Jessie. All of it."

Jessie hadn't known there was an "idiot" outside. She'd watched Reece leave. Who was out there?

"How do you know?" she asked.

"All those flashing lights were pretty obvious. I checked out your girlfriends' houses, and feeling satisfied you weren't there, came back to the neighborhood—just in time to see the light show. I parked a few streets down and came in through the back, over the neighbor's wall. Easy as apple pie on the Fourth of July, which by the way, is my favorite holiday."

"Go to hell."

"Already there. But I'll buy a first class ticket out as soon as you tell me why he's watching the house."

"I don't know. Probably because of you."

"Of course, but what proof did you give them? They didn't just believe your ramblings, I'm sure. You gave them something tangible. What?" Jack caressed her cheek with his Glock, keeping it close to her face. It was so close her eyes couldn't even focus on it. It smelled acrid, like it had been used recently.

Can people faint from being this afraid?

"Tell me or you die—and I still escape. I'm leaving one way or another, with or without you dead. Your choice."

Jessie didn't really believe the keeping-her-alive part. Why did Reece leave, anyway? Who was outside? She had trusted Reece Cannon. Maybe she couldn't believe anyone. Maybe she should scream.

Her entire world had been constructed with blatant lies.

And no one seemed to be helping. Her survival instincts were on high gear, but what could she really do?

Perhaps Jack would let her live if she told him everything about the phone.

But probably not.

Her best chance was the idiot outside.

"Okay, Jack. I'll tell you." Jessie prepared to scream at the top of her lungs.

Jack lowered the gun and took one step back, his dimples accentuating the smile returning to his face.

*   *   *

Hawk Kelly drove like a madman to Jack's address. He couldn't wait to get there and put an end to two problems with the elimination of one man. He'd be a hero, again, at the CIA. However, the Iranian spy wasn't a problem *only* for the Americans. He'd be a hero for Saudi Arabia too.

When he arrived, he noticed someone in uniform walking in front of Jack's house. The man paced in one direction, then spun around and walked back the way he came.

That must be the damn Lieutenant Shanahan.

Hawk pulled up to the man and rolled his window down. "Lieutenant?"

The man looked somewhat relieved. "Yes. Hawk?"

Hawk growled. "Get out of here. Now. Why are you even here?"

"The danger. I couldn't let anyone get hurt on my watch. I'm sure you understand."

"I only understand you're gonna lose your job if you don't comply. Last chance."

Shanahan stared off in the distance. "Yes, sir." Then he walked off.

Hawk looked around. *Where's he going?*

"Where's your car?" Hawk called out.

"Uh…at that gas station around the corner."

Shaking his head in disbelief, Hawk watched the idiot amble away.

Hawk parked, drew his gun and crept up to the house. Even though Jessie was supposedly in there, there was no sign of anybody moving through the dimly lit interior. Only a light shone from the kitchen.

Jack's probably already in there interrogating Jessie right now.

It didn't matter to Hawk. He was going to do what he was going to do. And if Jack wasn't in there, he'd interrogate Jessie first.

Then he heard a loud scream from the kitchen area.

Knowing how to throw his weight around, Hawk kicked in the front door, stepped inside, and then felt his stomach pushing acid up his throat from all the greasy food he'd eaten.

Ah, but there he was—Jack, standing over poor little Jessie, taped to a kitchen chair.

While Hawk got his bearings, Jack fired first. That first bullet splintered a hole into the front door.

Hawk didn't ask questions either. He fired back. Normally he was a good shot, but there's just something about acid reflux that messes with one's aim.

Jack dodged the bad shot, and the bullet went through the kitchen wall.

Bang!

Hawk felt a thudding pain in his belly, the force knocking him backwards. The second bullet Jack let loose had hit Hawk straight in his bulletproof Kevlar vest.

My goddamned stomach.

Jessie screamed again.

Hawk recovered and quickly pumped out a few more rounds, but Jack jumped back, retreating, vanishing from sight.

12

MAYBE IT WAS THE MAN that busted in her house and almost shot her, or the ensuing fireworks in her kitchen blowing out her ears, but Jessie's nerves unraveled. She could only think about death. She felt it near.

Her chest vibrated from screaming with intensity she didn't know she had, but she couldn't hear the sound of her voice. All she heard was ringing in her ears.

In front of her stood a clean-shaven, rounded man. He wore light-gray sweat pants that sported a few grease spots, and a brown aviator jacket over what must've been a bulletproof vest.

"Please help me," Jessie mouthed.

Jessie's kitchen opened to the living room on one end and to a hallway leading to bedrooms from the other end. Jack had run out of the kitchen and down the hallway while the round man approached from the living room.

"What do you know about Jamshid?" the man demanded of Jessie, without any effort of removing the duct tape fastening her to the chair.

Jessie could barely make out the words he said. Everything sounded muted. "Jack? I don't know anything, I swear."

"Don't lie to me! Or else—"

And then someone else entered her home, also with a gun. But this man was different. He wore a sheriff's deputy uniform. He charged in just in time to hear the man threaten her.

And he wasted no time.

*   *   *

Lieutenant Shanahan had been on the phone with Reece when he heard the scream and shots fired inside the home. He hadn't gone anywhere even though Hawk had told him to do so.

Shanahan hadn't the slightest inclination to leave until he knew Jessie would be absolutely safe. Shanahan didn't give a damn who told him what, especially that jerk who smelled like a deep fryer.

So when the sound of bullets started popping like popcorn, Shanahan was ready and running. And when he heard Deep Fryer Hawk threaten a duct-taped woman who he assumed to be Jessie, who was also stunningly beautiful, Shanahan decided it was time for him to do his job. He was the law around these parts.

But he felt a twinge of confusion. *Who is this guy? Did CIA really do that kind of thing to civilians? No, there's no way this is lawful on American soil.*

"Drop your weapon! Do it slowly!" Shanahan yelled.

Shanahan held his gun steady, pointed directly at Hawk—or whoever he was.

Quicker than he looked, Hawk maneuvered behind Jessie's chair and pressed his gun to her temple. Shanahan watched as Jessie's eyes closed, squeezing tears down her delicate face.

The pain or fear—or both—on this woman's face was palpable and hurt Shanahan in a way that went deep. There was something about her. This time it wasn't his brain that thought it; he felt it.

"Who are you, really?" Shanahan demanded.

"This is your last chance to walk away, or she dies. Right here, right now. The blood is on your hands, Lieutenant."

"If you shoot her, you die." Shanahan gritted his teeth.

"You're a sharpshooter?" Hawk snorted. "One of us has a vest. The other doesn't. I'm willing to wager you can't pull it off." Then he scowled, irritated. "And I'm outta time. Gotta get Jack. You have to the count of three. One, two…"

Shanahan knew something that Hawk didn't: Reece was on the way. He thought of her in that split-second.

It's on you now, Reece.

"Okay, you win." Shanahan slowly set his gun on the floor. He held his hands up, empty.

*   *   *

Reece made the ten-minute drive in five. Any quicker and she would've rolled her SUV off the corkscrewed, desert roads that wound around the base of the foothills.

She kept her lights and sirens quiet as she raced down Jessie's street. Reece had already placed the call for additional backup, but as the closest deputies had responded to her prior call to Prasan's house, the now-closest deputies were a few minutes behind her.

Shanahan was nowhere to be seen.

Barely parked, she lunged from the SUV and ran up to the house. The blinds were shut. She peered in the kitchen window, through a tiny hole in the closed blinds where the pull string went through, her nose smashed to the outside screen, pressing it against the glass.

Jessie was taped to a chair, and a big man had Shanahan sitting next to her, waving a gun around at them both. Was that Jack?

"Before you kill me, *Hawk*, at least tell me your real name," Shanahan said with no fear, staring at the man.

"C'mon, you think I'm some B-movie villain? You should've followed orders better." Hawk aimed his gun directly at Shanahan, about to take the kill shot.

Reece had gotten there just in time.

She fired through the window. Although Reece could hit a quarter at fifty yards, she didn't hit Hawk. He stood too close to Jessie and Shanahan, and Reece didn't chance an accident. She missed on purpose.

The window shattered and the distraction worked. Hawk lost focus and quickly turned toward the window, taking a shot.

Reece had already dove down and away, rolling on the ground. Then up, she sprinted towards the front door.

Hawk's distraction lasted long enough for Shanahan to reach out and knock the gun in his hand sideways. Then Shanahan tackled him. They both crashed to the floor, wrestling for the gun.

Reece made her way inside the house, just as Hawk used his weight to pin Shanahan. Reece might not have another chance to miss on purpose. At least Jessie, the civilian, was at a safe enough distance to not be hit.

Reece aimed for his arm and fired. But Hawk had been moving. His body jerked left right then.

The world stopped moving for a moment as Reece watched a small blood stain appear on the side of Hawk's head. What came out the other side wasn't pretty. The body immediately went limp, briefly falling on Shanahan before he shoved the lifeless mass off.

Unable to peel her eyes from the dead man—a dead CIA agent?—Reece tried to shake off the shock of the accidental kill. The lights seemed brighter. The air smelled stronger. Her knees wobbled and she felt sick.

Then Shanahan jumped to his feet and lunged at Reece, knocking her backwards, inches from the still-open front door. Reece felt her standard issue slip from her hands to the floor.

Another shot rang out. Jack had appeared. He fired again at them while they scrambled on the ground, rolling out the front door.

"Jessie," Shanahan whispered as they rolled into the cool night air.

Jack's firing ceased.

Reece's instincts took over, not giving her any more time to be sick. But Jack didn't come after them.

Reece heard Jessie scream something from inside. Jack must've been going after her first, probably tying up loose ends while he had the chance.

Shanahan moved closer to the front door. "If I can get in there, my gun's still on the floor."

"Don't. Did you save Jack's number?" Reece asked.

"I remember it."

"Call him."

13

SHANAHAN IMMEDIATELY CLICKED a voice-recording app on his phone and dialed Jack's iPhone while jogging out of earshot, over to Reece's SUV. He noticed a few neighbors had emerged from their homes, probably because of the gunshots. Shanahan motioned for everybody to stay back.

I hope my accent is convincing enough.

Reece stayed by the front door, keeping a close eye on the situation. Shanahan desperately wanted to charge in there and get Jessie out. Every bone in his body knew Jack would shoot her at any moment.

Finally, Jack answered.

Speaking in Farsi, Shanahan spoke urgently. "Jamshid, abort. No more killing. We've been found out. We need to handle the situation differently."

"Abort, now? Who is this?" Jack asked, more submissive than Shanahan would've thought possible.

Shanahan looked up at the stars hoping he'd say the right thing. "This is the one who handles people who make mistakes."

Jack paused for a second before responding. "I can take care of it. Let me clean this up."

"Too many people know." Shanahan took a leap of faith. "They know you killed the Deputy Executive Director. Why did you make such a mistake?"

"He knew too much. I had to…"

Gotcha.

Jack continued. "I had to eliminate anything that led back to the mission." His tone started to sound apologetic. "Everything for the mission."

As Shanahan listened, he glanced at the time.

Where the hell is backup?

* * *

Jamshid Darbandi was moments away from killing Jessie and going after the annoying deputies. His mission might be compromised, but Hawk—no doubt the Saudi informant—bleeding all over the floor meant that Jamshid had championed another success.

And perhaps this new success might convince his agency to let him continue, to let him fix this. He could still take control of the situation.

But, a new agent spoke to him—someone who "handles people who make mistakes."

This was not good news for Jamshid.

The new voice told him "no more killing."

Jamshid stared at his fiancée, who looked like a mental basketcase. Her hair was messed, her eyes were red and puffy, and she was appalling to gaze upon. Jamshid always hated her emotional nonsense. She couldn't handle anything. If he'd been choosing freely, he would've never chosen such a woman for himself.

"Leave everything now. Do you hear me?" The voice on the other end of the line said.

"I can correct this small error! I only have to—"

"All you have to do is disappear," the voice said. "Now!"

"Yes, I will," Jamshid forced out through gritted teeth. "But mark my words: before tonight is over, only those who know me as Special Agent Jack will survive, I promise you." And with those words, Jamshid tucked Reece's gun—which he had picked up moments ago—into his belt, and bolted for the back door.

"Wait!" yelled the voice.

Jamshid hadn't yet hung up the phone. He returned the little speaker to his ear as he made his way to the backyard.

The voice spoke English. "Jamshid, FYI, you're busted. You have the right to remain silent…"

Jamshid smashed the *End Call* button and ripped the gun from his belt.

*   *   *

Reece heard Shanahan switch to English, got a thumbs-up from him, and then she immediately rushed the house. She looked, but her gun was no longer on the living room floor.

In the kitchen, Jessie sat alone, save for a chocolate Labrador retriever at her feet with its paws on her lap. The sound of footsteps towards the back alerted Reece to Jack's whereabouts, and she chased after him with Shanahan a few strides behind. On the way she snatched a gun from the kitchen counter—not hers, but it would give her protection.

Rounding a hallway, Reece barely had a microsecond to register a gun firing at her. She ducked back but the bullet grazed her left arm, near her shoulder.

"Drop it! You're under arrest!" she yelled, barely registering the pain.

No one dropped anything. Instead, she heard the click of a deadbolt.

High on adrenaline, Reece couldn't feel the wound. She reached around the corner and fired a shot, but it didn't take. She then withdrew her extended hand and ducked while simultaneously pushing Shanahan back, out of the way of returned bullets going straight through the hallway drywall.

When Jack ceased firing, it sounded like he next opened the back door. Reece leapt out of the hallway, into the room with a dive towards the ground.

The world seemed to slow down just like how it did when she got in fights as an angsty teenager. Back then, she had even scrapped against boys, since girl fights were no fun. Whenever her opponent started swinging, their arms and fists seemed to be moving in molasses. The entire world slowed down for her.

Reece had dodged blows and responded with quick fists. It seemed fictitious, borderline silly to explain to someone, but her swiftness under pressure was an unusual trait.

She still had it.

As she flew to the floor in slow motion, she identified her target and pulled the trigger. The bullet splintered through the back door as it slammed shut behind Jack, who had dashed out into the backyard.

Reece landed on the floor. Her left shoulder hit first, her injury stinging. A quick tuck and roll later, she sprang to her feet, her muscles coiled like a tightly wound spring. She flung the back door open, and a few bounds later, she lunged at Jack, smashing into his body in the open night air.

14

MAISIE'S MIND WAS RACING, replaying the events that had led her to this moment. She could still see Jack's face, twisted with determination as he peeped through her windows, banged on the front door—absolutely 100% searching for Jessie.

Maisie hadn't answered the door, having her own inklings about Jack's lies, which Jessie had still only half-told her about. So instead, she'd watched him leave, her curiosity piqued and suspicion ignited like a spark in the dry brush.

She trailed his Maserati through the quiet streets, her eyes narrowed in concentration. When Jack parked on the street behind his and Jessie's home, alarm bells rang in her head. Why would he choose such an odd approach? Her gut screamed that something huge was amiss.

The past blended into the present as Maisie sat in her car, the engine idling. She'd been there for what felt like an eternity, her fingers drumming an anxious rhythm on the steering wheel, her eyes flitting between the rearview mirror and her phone.

She dialed Jessie's number, but the call rang through to voicemail, leaving her even more unsettled. Should she interfere? Was this meddling or protecting her friend? The questions swirled in her mind, each one more insistent than the last.

The silence of indecision was finally shattered as Maisie took a deep breath and made up her mind. "Screw it," she muttered.

She stepped out of her car and strode purposefully towards the neighbor's backyard, her eyes on the prize: the truth about Jack. But when she neared the fence separating the yards, a gunshot split the night like a thunderclap.

*   *   *

After Reece had launched herself at Jack, Shanahan then lunged at Jack too, and that's when all three of them went down.

At first, Reece barely registered Shanahan's phone fall out of his pocket. But she realized it in full effect when Jack zeroed in on it, and instead of firing at the deputies—he fired at the phone instead.

A direct hit, the phone screen completely shattered and the phone itself was visibly destroyed.

Reece knew exactly what that meant. The proof they had gotten when Shanahan recorded Jack may now be gone.

She desperately needed Jack's iPhone lookalike. That fake was definitive proof of who he was.

Jack swung the butt of his gun at Reece. She dodged the attack, raising her own gun and training it on Jack's chest. But before she could pull the trigger, Jack's foot connected with her wrist, sending her weapon flying through the air.

Shanahan then threw his body over Jack's, the men colliding like freight trains. The air crackled with violence as they grappled, each trying to gain the upper hand.

The struggle was vicious. Jack's elbow found its mark on Shanahan's temple, the impact swift and brutal. Shanahan crumpled to the ground, unconscious and vulnerable.

"Shan!" Reece cried, torn between pursuing Jack and tending to her fallen partner and friend. She knelt by his side, her fingers trembling as they traced the angry welt blossoming on his forehead.

Suddenly the chocolate Lab came bounding into the backyard, barking furiously. The dog was surely confused at the situation, racing towards its owner.

In that moment of distraction, Jack seized the opportunity to flee, vaulting over the back cinderblock wall. The dog kept barking incessantly, jumping and going crazy.

But that wasn't the end of the horrific situation.

A woman had appeared a second earlier, peeking her head over the wall and calling out, "Jessie!? Are you o—"

Jack slapped his hand over her mouth. He dragged her backwards, her muffled screaming quickly fading.

Jack could be heard grunting from the neighbor's backyard, "Shut your mouth, Maisie."

Reece dashed for the gun Jack had kicked away from her, plucking it from the ground. Then she sprinted after him, scaling the fence.

Jack paused his escape when he saw her, placing his gun against Maisie's head. "Come any closer and she's dead!" he called out.

Reece stood there, her mind racing as to the correct course of action. She couldn't take the chancy shot. She could only hope he'd let Maisie go.

The two disappeared, out to the street beyond the neighbor's house.

Reece ran after them, darting from the yard just in time to see Jack's black Maserati screaming away. And there was no sight of Maisie anywhere. Reece was left with nothing but the woman's phantom screams to haunt her.

What have I done?

All Reece wanted to do was help Jessie, who was being played by a fake fiancé, and in doing so, fulfill her own dream of saving the world.

That's what it was, wasn't it? Some grand idea that had no merit or basis in reality?

Now, because of her, Jessie's dad, a Deputy Executive Director of the CIA, had been murdered, and Maisie had been abducted as an impromptu hostage. Maisie's life was obviously in jeopardy.

It was all Reece's fault for jumping the gun, being too green, too naïve.

Whether her intention had been right or wrong, Reece suddenly felt a wave of shame. The thought of rescuing Maisie safely was the only lifeline she had to keep her from falling off this mental and emotional cliff she teetered on the edge of.

And then she heard the sirens behind her—the backup she had requested earlier. She heard several deputies run into Jessie's backyard, and one of them looked over the fence, spotting Reece. But this deputy wasn't just anyone; Reece recognized him as Captain Jeff Prestwood, a seasoned officer with a lot of sway and experience.

"What the hell!?" he yelled at Reece. "You had no authorization for doing any of this! And you killed the man in the living room?—you're in deep shit! Get your ass back here and give me your badge! You're suspended, effective immediately!"

15

THE RELIEF JESSIE EXPERIENCED when Jack had run off, leaving her alive and bullet-free, felt immeasurable.

But she was still taped to the chair, and deputies were currently pouring into her home like ants on an anthill.

Then, from the backyard, that first deputy walked in again—the one who tried to save her—and he quickly strode up to her. He gave the other deputies, who had crowded around her, a look. They walked off, leaving the two of them in the kitchen alone.

"Ma'am, I'm so sorry this is all happening," he said as he finished cutting the tape from her body. "If there's anything I can do…"

Jessie looked at the welt on the side of his head, no doubt the result of a physical fight with Jack. It needed tending to.

"What's your name?" she asked.

Maybe it was being rescued from death, maybe it was the flood of emotions that wouldn't stop, but regardless, there was something safe and magnetic about this man's presence.

"Oh, sorry... Tommy. Lieutenant Tommy Shanahan with Pima County."

Jessie smiled a little before tearing up again. She stood and stretched a bit, but didn't break eye contact. The freedom to move felt amazing, something she would never take for granted again.

"I, ah, I'm just glad you're safe, ma'am." Shanahan continued looking at her, and she stared right back, examining his green eyes.

"I have some...bad news, ma'am."

"What could possibly be worse than this?"

"Your father..."

Jessie's legs gave out and she fell to the floor in a heap. The news was just too much to take. Shanahan crouched down and tried to comfort her.

She banged on his chest, pounding on him as though if she beat him hard enough, what he said might not be true. He let her pound until she couldn't lift her hands anymore.

After she was done, he gently placed his arms around her in a hug-like gesture, and she fell into him, soaking his button-up in tears.

16

JESSIE STOOD AT THE DESERT'S EDGE near her home, shivering as the chill of the night set in around her. Despite the discomfort, she remained still, feeling an unshakable dread at the thought of returning to her defiled home. She was utterly terrified.

As a child, her dad half-whispered "made up" stories—*yeah, right*—about CIA operatives and foreign spies. They stirred her soul again, now.

The light breeze carried the scent of sagebrush, momentarily transporting her back to a time when life was simpler. A time before she realized the world was full of deceit. She yearned for the stress and pain to disappear.

Jessie's sole agenda had been a simple one: she just wanted to live a normal life, whatever that is. At least something that resembled normal. She had no interest in the clandestine worldly issues her dad was obsessed with. Rather, *had been* obsessed with.

All she wanted was to feel safe, to stay as far away from Jack as possible, and now, perhaps even Reece.

Jessie glanced down at the furry guy next to her. Its tongue lolled out of its mouth, its eyes wide with excitement. She patted Coco's head, feeling the soft fur under her hand. She smiled despite the chaos around them—a small comfort in a world gone mad.

She looked up, gazing at the mountain's silhouettes in the distance. Her thoughts drifted to an episode of some random show she had seen years ago. The episode was about an amateur cryptographer who received an encrypted message with a note saying that the secret to a hidden treasure was locked within the puzzle. Intrigued, the cryptographer dedicated weeks to deciphering the code.

As the cryptographer worked tirelessly on the puzzle, he began to decipher parts of the message. But each revelation only led to more questions, and the cryptographer fell deeper and deeper into the mystery.

The desert's silence was interrupted by the distant howl of a coyote, jolting Jessie back to her present reality. The juxtaposition of the lighthearted show and her current predicament was not lost on her, and she found herself pondering the two extremes.

On one hand, imagining herself becoming further involved in this nightmare felt impossible, paralyzing. Her dream of a normal life was slipping through her fingers like the cryptographer's puzzle pieces.

On the other hand, as Jessie gazed at the moonlit wisps of clouds shimmering above, her thoughts turned to Reece Cannon. She'd seemed like she'd really cared, but Jessie remained confused and apprehensive about the deputy's motivations.

Did she really need to bring her dad into this? His murder was her fault, wasn't it? Jessie's trauma had left her broken, unable to see beyond her own fears and desires. Was she like the cryptographer in that episode?

When the cryptographer finally unlocked the last piece of the puzzle and excitedly read the message in its entirety, he found that the message, it turned out, was a series of simple, almost mundane instructions.

The punchline of the joke was that the hidden treasure turned out to be a recipe for the world's best grilled cheese sandwich. The cryptographer had spent weeks deciphering a code, only to be rewarded with a recipe for the simplest of comfort foods. Jessie couldn't help but laugh out loud, the absurdity of it providing a welcome break from the heaviness of her situation.

She wiped away a tear, thinking about the grilled cheese sandwiches her dad used to make. Sure, he hadn't been around much, but he had cared. He had loved the best he knew how. And damn, he had made some good comfort food. What she wouldn't do for another one of his sandwiches right now.

With a deep breath, she turned to head back to her home, knowing full well that the circus of police cars and deputies, red and blue lights, and yellow caution tape would be waiting for her. She could only hope that the pressures of the outside world wouldn't shatter what was left of her fragile mental state.

*   *   *

Jack hadn't set fire to Jessie's life with one single match. It had been a slow burn, a slow unraveling that had taken almost getting married to fully manifest.

Now, as Reece left the sheriff's department—without her badge—she could feel the weight of Jack's influence also bearing down on her.

Her clothes were disheveled and her shoulder bloody. She had washed her face in the bathroom sink, but her neck and the sides of her face still felt sticky from sweat and dirt.

As she drove home, her mind drifted back to the moments that had brought her to this desolate place. Captain Jeff Prestwood and her peers had shown up to find a dead body—*a CIA agent!?*—lying on the ground, *shot down by yours truly.*

Everything had escalated so fast.

But Hawk's actions—they didn't add up, just like Jack's hadn't.

She remembered Shanahan's words to her: *You're a rookie, Reece. Nothing smells right to you.*

Could she even trust her own instincts?

Yet, how could she simply quit now, when a life was on the line and every second mattered?—even if Captain Prestwood had taken her badge.

What would they all do anyway? Go on fishing trips? Go home for dinner? Write a goddamn report, first, before doing anything about Maisie's abduction?

Reece literally slapped herself while driving. She had to pull it together.

She had thought Jessie was the emotional one, but was Reece faring any better? She had to fix this—and fix herself.

At least, that's what she told herself. Maybe she was still trying to shake the discombobulating and sickening feeling of killing someone.

Reece had to keep moving forward, keep pushing.

The chaos in Reece's mind broke a memory loose, like a fragment of a shattered mirror reflecting one of the faces of her past.

As she pulled her Jeep into the driveway of her home, she remembered it now.

One morning, as Reece got to her high school, she noticed a woman, a mom of some other student, her face etched with fear and apprehension. The woman's boyfriend loomed over her, his dirty presence a dark cloud suffocating the air around her. Reece's instincts screamed that something was amiss, but what could she do?

A teacher walked by, calling out to Reece, "Get to class, people, let's go!" The clock was ticking, the hands of fate urging her to obey. But as she glanced back at the woman, that instinctual feeling refused to leave, and she knew that she couldn't just walk away.

Reece had her mom's old car parked in the school's student parking lot. In an act of defiance, she bolted for the car and took off, following the woman and her boyfriend.

Long story short, the woman's distress led Reece down a path she never could have imagined. It turned out the boyfriend was using her to peddle hard drugs, and was having her drive him around while doing it.

Reece ended up calling the police. Later, as the handcuffs clicked around the boyfriend's wrists, Reece knew that she had made the right choice even though it took breaking the rules to do it.

But as the memories of that fateful day faded, Reece found herself haunted by the ghosts of her instincts. Her rebellious nature had risen like a phoenix from the ashes, threatening to engulf her world in flames. Every heroic deed has its price, and the reckoning was upon her.

Reece hadn't moved from her Jeep. She sat there with the engine off. Yet, the world around her felt like a blur of colors and sounds, a cacophony of pandemonium and confusion. She tried to think clearly.

In order to find Maisie, she'd have to find Jack. And to find Jack, she needed to speak with Jessie. If anybody knew where Jack could be, even if it was buried in her subconscious, was Jessie; perhaps there was a clue or some detail in her memory that Reece could see in a new light.

Am I really doing this?

I can't, she silently told herself.

But how could she not?

Reece needed the courage to grow beyond her naïveté. That much was for sure.

If something happened to Maisie, the only way she'd be able to live with herself was to have seen this all the way through. Despite the barriers in her path, she needed to take action.

17

CHIEF CARLOS GOMEZ leaned forward, still in plainclothes, his hands clenched tightly on the desk as he stared at Sheriff Luke Landy with a steely gaze.

It neared 11:00 PM on Thursday, and they were both in the office, eye to eye, looking pissed.

"What fire do you need me to put out now?" Gomez asked, not bothering to hide his irritation. He had barely managed to get the fish in the freezer before being called in—all the while still supposedly on vacation.

Landy sighed heavily before responding. "It's not good, Carlos. A CIA agent named Jack Darbandi, an alleged Iranian foreign intelligence agent—crazy, right?—is missing. Not only that, Jack's acting director was murdered in his own home earlier tonight. And if that wasn't enough, a second CIA operative was murdered in Jack's own living room—but not by Jack. There are even rumors that—"

Gomez's eyes widened in shock. "What? I go on a little fishing trip and all this? I knew I should've stayed at the *puto* lake."

Landy replied. "But there's something else we need to discuss," Landy replied. "That's why I wanted you here. It's about one of our own."

¡No mames! Gomez growled. "You're telling me we got a missing CIA agent who's possibly a double agent, two dead ones, and on top of all that, now there's talk that one of our own is involved?"

Landy nodded grimly. "And that rookie, I think you know her—Reece Cannon—she's at the center of it all."

Gomez was taken aback. "You're kidding me, right? She seems like a bright kid."

Landy shifted uncomfortably in his seat, his gaze darting around the room. "Personally, I don't know much about her," he admitted. "What exactly do you mean by 'bright'?"

Gomez leaned forward, his voice serious. "You know damn well what I mean, Luke. What's the word on what really happened at Jessie's house?"

Landy's voice dropped to a harsh whisper. "The word from our guys is that Reece Cannon killed a CIA Agent named Hawk Kelly. Captain Prestwood showed up after, confirmed the situation, and then suspended her." Landy leaned back in his chair. "Not. Looking. Good."

"That's some straight up BS," Gomez spat. "Nothing's solid until we get proof. Some weird shit went down."

"There's witnesses," Landy said, his voice laced with doubt. "Even Lieutenant Shanahan confirmed it. He was there in the room when the CIA agent was shot by Reece."

Gomez squinted at Landy, giving him a look that said: *What's the rest of the story?*

"Although," Landy emphasized, "Shanahan claims Reece 'protected' him—hell, maybe she did. I don't know. Maybe they were mistaken. I don't know what anybody thought. But from my standpoint, details are sketchy, and there's gonna be hell to pay regardless of assumptions *anyone* had."

Gomez scowled. "I'm beginning to understand that we know a whole lot of nothing right now," he said, his voice firm. "We can't jump to conclusions. If Reece had a lawful reason, we'll make damn sure her name is cleared."

Landy nodded in agreement. "Agreed. But we also need to consider the possibility that the rookie didn't. And if she's guilty, she'll have to be brought to justice."

Gomez's jaw tightened as he stood up from his chair. "We'll do what we have to do," he said, his voice cold and resolute. "Our main focus right now should be figuring out what the hell is really going down. Where is Jack?—do we have him here for questioning?"

"That's the other thing," Landy explained. "Reece claims Jack took a hostage and drove off in a black Maserati—said it has a big spoiler on it. Should be easy to spot. We have an APB out for it now."

"This is getting uglier by the second."

"Now you're seeing what I'm seeing. Hawk could very well have been there for Jack, and Reece messed up bad."

Gomez groaned. "Where is Shanahan or Reece now?"

*   *   *

Shanahan moved with purpose, his eyes scanning the landscape for any sign of Jack or Maisie.

He tried calling Reece again, but it just went to voicemail. Problem was, his phone had been destroyed, and the one he was using right now would look like an unknown number to her; she wouldn't know it was him calling.

Plus, he didn't blame her for not wanting to talk to anyone. Despite his contrary testimony, he couldn't wrap his head around the idea that Captain Prestwood took her badge.

Although Shanahan wanted to believe that his sheriff's department was a beacon of infallible truth, he knew that the political ramifications of a CIA agent being shot and killed by one of Sheriff Landy's deputies meant that the bureaucratic red tape was coming out in full force.

It seemed like the whole department was converging against the rookie. Even still, Shanahan was not about to give up on his old friend, regardless of who Hawk was or wasn't.

Hawk had been in the wrong. His tactics had been completely unbelievable and suspect. Shanahan didn't believe he was putting on 'an act' for one second.

The night sky was cloudy, just like Shanahan's mood.

His senses were heightened to their fullest extent as he jogged. The moonlight illuminated the desert terrain, casting unsettling shadows across the earth. He listened intently, straining to hear any sound that might lead him in the right direction. But the crunch of gravel beneath his boots was the only thing that broke the silence.

The buzz from the double shot of whiskey, over three hours ago, had long since worn off, and he had downed a pot's worth of coffee too.

Since then, he had been driving to different locals and getting out of his vehicle to search by foot. He had checked some nearby industrial spots, and now currently searched some of the undeveloped patches dotting the landscape between the populated areas.

The smell of the desert filled his nostrils—dry earth, cactus, and the occasional whiff of sage. He could see the outline of the mountains in the distance, their jagged peaks looking like they were made of black paper cutouts against the night sky.

As he searched, his thoughts turned to the Iranian government. He fully believed that Jack was a dangerous man, posed a significant threat, and that he would stop at nothing to protect himself. Furthermore, Shanahan couldn't discount the possibility that other Iranian operatives were here too, possibly to aid Jack. Things could get much worse.

Despite the potential for impending disaster, he couldn't help but think of Reece's bullheaded fortitude. She was a woman of true grit. He felt proud for having stood by her side earlier.

Shanahan gave one last look around. This search wasn't going anywhere. If Jack was smart—which he no doubt was—he would've switched cars anyway. Finding a needle in a haystack was exactly what this felt like.

It was high time to do an investigation of his own. He had found Hawk's wallet and a driver's license in the car Hawk had driven, and then memorized the man's home address. He would go there now and see what he could find.

Even if the CIA had people there, or the FBI had already shown, he was still a lieutenant, and as such, had responsibilities to investigate any violent crimes in the entire county. Legally, they couldn't keep him out.

*   *   *

Reece's pulse raced as she dialed Jessie's number. She was keenly aware of the stakes and her need for secrecy.

Jessie picked up on the third ring, her voice shaking. "Reece?" she whispered.

"Jessie, listen to me," Reece urged. "I need your help. Can you talk?"

There was a pause on the other end of the line. Finally, she spoke. "I don't know what to say."

"Jessie, what exactly are you talking about?"

There was another pause, and then her voice broke. "I didn't know what to say to Captain Prestwood. He was pressuring me about you. I'm…so confused."

"Where was Shanahan when this happened?"

"He went looking for you."

Reece thought about what that all really meant. The probability of things getting worse was a lot higher than getting better. And if no one caught Jack soon, he could flee the country—most likely killing his final victim beforehand.

"I need you to focus, Jessie," Reece said firmly. "Do you know where Jack is? I know you think you don't know, but wrack your brain for things he said or did, or maybe that you saw—things that don't add up, no matter how inconsequential something may seem. Any places he frequents, or friends, or anything?"

"I don't think so…"

Reece calmly talked with her for another minute or so, asking about different topics. Finally, she got somewhere.

"Wait," Jessie recalled, "I found a business card in Jack's office for a storage facility, like, six or seven months ago. Um, Tucson Self Storage, I think. Maybe that's relevant?"

"That's golden, Jessie. Any clue on the unit number?"

"There was a number written on the back. Fifty-six," she relayed, her voice shaking. "I only remember because that was the year my"—her voice trailed before coming back in—"the year my…dad was born."

Reece could hear Jessie choke back emotion before continuing. "But Reece, I don't want anything to happen to Maisie. Please…she has such a good heart. If anything happens to her…"

"Everyone's on it," Reece stated. "We're going to find her."

After the call ended, Reece knew what she had to do. She had a possible lead. But she had to be careful, she had to be smart, and she had to not get arrested by her own department.

Time to get to work.

18

SHERIFF LUKE LANDY sat in his office, the telephone on his desk buzzing like an angry hornet, demanding his attention. It was time to take a call he didn't want to take.

"David," Sheriff Landy's voice crackled through the line, a hint of irritation apparent, "what can I do for you?"

The voice of the Executive Director of the CIA, David Pomeroy—not only Hawk's superior, but Prasan's superior as well—held the urgency of a telemarketer on commission. "Have you arrested that rogue deputy, Reece Cannon, yet?"

"Arrested?" Landy cleared his throat. "Ah…not exactly. But the investigation is ongoing. We've dealt with justifiable homicide before."

"Justifiable?" David scoffed, a dark chuckle sounding over the line. "Oh, this is much worse than that, my friend. One of my best agents is dead. If you don't find Reece, and I mean yesterday, every goddamn agency from the CIA to the FBI to the ATF is gonna rain down on your county like the hammer of Thor."

"Jesus, David. I have a respected lieutenant that says—"

"Let me interrupt you, Landy. Get your boots on the ground and bring her in, and charge her, immediately."

"You're serious, huh?"

"Do I sound like I'm joking?" David's voice was quiet, but no less powerful for it. "See that you do this in a quick manner, or you'll be able to count your remaining days as sheriff on one hand. Do I make myself clear?"

*   *   *

Captain Jeff Prestwood was a towering figure, both in height and authority, with a no-nonsense approach to law enforcement. His gruff demeanor and firm jawline commanded respect from his subordinates, and his deep baritone voice could rattle even the most hardened criminals.

Currently, Captain Prestwood stood across the desk from one of his deputies, his voice carrying the weight of his austerity. "You need to secure that arrest warrant, now, and make sure the affidavit is tighter than a corset on a Sunday morning. We can't afford any mistakes in this case. Sheriff Landy was clear on this: Reece needs to be brought back in for questioning and charged with voluntary manslaughter."

The deputy nodded as he typed Reece's name on the form with the official charges next to it.

Captain Prestwood scanned the deputy's computer screen. "Make sure you present the judge with solid evidence, including witness testimony from Jessie, and statements from law enforcement regarding Reece's actions, taking on the case alone and unsupervised. We need to make sure the judge agrees there's probable cause to believe Reece committed this crime."

"I'll make sure everything is in order," the deputy said, his fingers tapping the keyboard.

"Let me know the second we get a response." Then: "And where the hell did Lieutenant Shanahan rustle off to? I'm *this close* to suspending his ass too. I want him off this case immediately."

"Yes, sir, I'll radio for him to come in."

Captain Prestwood strode off, his mind whirring with this night's slipshod malarkey. They had to be careful, meticulous, and thorough in their investigation. The stakes were higher than a rodeo bucking bull in Las Vegas.

*   *   *

Reece walked into her home, going straight to her bedroom closet. The ticking of a clock in her head seemed to echo like her footfalls on the wood flooring.

She wanted to inspect the storage facility, but first, she changed into a black t-shirt and dark pair of jeans. Forgoing a shower, she ducked her head in the sink and squeezed the grime out of her shoulder-length blonde hair.

She checked the bandage just below her left shoulder; it was fine. She still had 90% functionality with her arm.

I'm right-handed anyway.

Her mind was a blur, calculating the minutes since last seeing Maisie being dragged off. Time was slipping away, and every moment mattered.

The world seemed to slow down as she took a deep breath, steeling herself for what lay ahead. She could already feel the adrenaline pumping through her veins, urging her to move.

She opened her safe and removed a weapon, the same type as her standard issue from the sheriff's department—a Glock 19. Fifteen rounds in the clip. She tucked it into a concealed carry holster on her waistline.

Out in the garage, she grabbed a pair of bolt cutters.

A few moments later, she was sitting back in her Jeep and starting the engine.

*   *   *

Ethan Wilson stood with another deputy in Jessie's living room, where Hawk was killed. Though the deputy had a year of service on Ethan, he was a foot shorter and weighed about half as much, and seemed to be the nerdy type, which was the complete opposite of brawny Ethan.

"I wish I would've eaten before coming here," Ethan grumbled. "I won't be able to scarf down anything for a few hours after seeing this bloody mess."

"I don't think you'll have much of a problem," the other deputy replied.

"Yeah, actually, I am pretty hungry." Ethan's face turned sour. "Do you think it's fair that Landy's trying to hang Reece for this?" he asked.

The other deputy did a lazy neck role. "If she broke the law, then yeah," he answered while doing another neck role in the opposite direction. "But it'll be crazy if one of our own is charged with manslaughter, or worse, murder."

"Listen, bro," Ethan said, his voice dropping to a low, conspiratorial tone. "I don't care what anyone says about Reece. Something isn't right here. The fact is, she's got more balls than any of us put together."

*   *   *

Captain Prestwood leaned back in his leather chair, studying the papers on his desk as a deputy approached him.

"What's the word?" he asked, looking up.

"We received the email from the on-call judge about the arrest warrant for Reece Cannon."

Prestwood let out a low whistle. "Well, I'll be damned. It won't be long now before we have Reece in here for questioning. Get someone to go to her house and escort her down here."

19

REECE CHECKED THE TIME—almost midnight. Every second she drove felt like the ticking of a bomb's timer.

A few minutes later, she pulled up to Tucson Self Storage, one of those outdoor places. Staying low key, she parked a little ways down the road, and then jogged back on foot.

Her eyes scanned the perimeter for any danger as she climbed over the entrance gate. She crept through the dimly lit storage facility, her ears hyper-aware of every noise or rustle in the shadows.

Approaching unit fifty-six, Reece sensed eyes on her. She couldn't shake the feeling that someone was there. She scanned the area, her attention darting from side to side, but saw nothing. Yet the feeling of being watched lingered like a bad omen.

Finally, Reece stood before Jack's unit. No signs of life, just a stubborn lock clinging to a chain on the door. Disappointment set in.

Nonetheless, she hefted the bolt cutters to the lock, squeezing the rubber grips together. With a little muscle, she snipped the metal and yanked the chain loose. Then she pulled open the roll-up door.

Inside, a metal safe and some plastic bins greeted her. Reece approached them, eager to uncover their secrets.

But before she could open one, she heard a sound behind her. A shuffling noise. She spun around.

That's when she saw him—a tall, menacing figure in the shadows. He stepped forward, locking eyes onto Reece.

"Who are you?" she demanded.

The man stepped forward again, his Persian accent thick and intimidating. "Tell me your name, and I'll tell you mine," he replied.

"Deputy Reece Cannon. You better have a damn good reason for being here."

The man's gaze remained steady. "It seems we're both here for the same reason. I'm looking for Jamshid Darbandi. You may know him as Jack."

"He's obviously not here," Reece said firmly. "And you still haven't told me your name."

The man simply quirked an eyebrow, like he was a scholar or philosopher about to share his great wisdom.

"The cleverest ruse of the devil," he said, "is to persuade you he does not exist." He smiled. "I am Cyrus Sasani. The one and only." Then he gave a small bow.

Reece smirked. "So dramatic."

She had her concealed gun, but after what had happened earlier, it was a last resort—especially because she was technically suspended right now. The last thing she needed was to kill someone else *before* getting them in an interrogation room.

Plus, she still had the bolt cutters in her hands, which made a pretty formidable weapon in and of itself.

The two circled each other, their eyes locked in a deadly stare. Cyrus made the first move, lunging towards Reece with a 6" knife. But Reece quickly sidestepped and kicked the back of Cyrus's knee, causing him to stumble.

As he regained his footing, she swung the bolt cutters towards his head, narrowly missing him as jumped backwards.

Cyrus surprised her though, reaching out and grabbing the bolt cutters, yanking them away, using the momentum to swing her to the ground. The bolt cutters also went flying.

She landed next to the metal chain that the lock had been connected to. She clamped it around her hand, and then sprang up, swinging it at him. But he ducked, and then kicked Reece in the stomach, causing her to tumble backwards.

But Reece wasn't finished yet. Finding herself next to one of the plastic bins, she grabbed a pair of pliers from atop and stabbed them into Cyrus's arm as he lunged at her again. He gasped in pain, but countered with a sharp elbow strike to her face.

Blood trickled down her nose, which Reece wiped with the back of her hand. Luckily, Cyrus had been off balance, or the blow could've been a lot worse.

He wasn't going down easy. She could no longer afford to hold back her best weapon.

She whipped out her Glock and leveled it at the man, ready to fire. "Get down on your knees and keep your hands where I can see them!"

Cyrus lunged at her, instead.

The shock of killing Hawk—still fresh and raw in her mind's eye—caused Reece to hesitate.

Cyrus tackled her to the ground, smacking the gun away. His hand closed around her throat.

Reece scrambled, panting for breath as she writhed in agony. In her struggle, she noticed a metal pipe on the ground. Reaching for it, she smashed it against Cyrus's ribs. He released his grip on her throat—but not before he had dragged his knife's edge down Reece's left forearm. Blood instantly poured from her arm.

She had to make a quick move before he recovered from the cracked ribs. Through one of the see-through bins, she saw a hammer. She sprang up and back, ripped the lid off, and reached inside.

As Cyrus got to his feet, looking as menacing as ever, Reece hurled the hammer at him with as much force as she could muster, like it was a throwing axe. The hammer impacted him straight on his right cheekbone with a sickening crunch.

The hammer clinked to the pavement as Cyrus dropped to his knees, cradling his face. Reece didn't wait to see the damage; she darted straight towards the exit gate.

*　　*　　*

Cyrus kneeled on the ground, dazed, spitting out blood and a few teeth. The hammer had broken his cheekbone and probably his eye socket too.

I have a job to do, he told himself.

I can't let a little girl stop me.

Yet as he struggled to get to his feet, with intense pain searing through his face and head, a presence fell across him. He looked up to see Jamshid Darbandi standing there with a grim expression. Cyrus knew what he needed to do; he had been ordered to kill Jamshid, and he wasn't going to back down now.

With a snarl, he lunged, but he was no match for the uninjured man's quick reflexes. Jamshid dodged his blows easily, and before Cyrus knew what was happening, he was lying on the ground again, this time with Jamshid's foot on his chest.

Cyrus struggled to catch his breath as Jamshid looked down at him with cold eyes. He realized too late what was about to happen. He heard the sound of a gunshot.

And that was it.

20

REECE, BLOODIED AND INJURED, thought long and hard about dialing 911.

She made a makeshift tourniquet and bandage from an extra shirt she had found in her Jeep. But it was rapidly soaking through, and she needed real bandaging, even stitches.

Her Jeep's tires were completely flat. It looked like sabotage.

The thought of being whisked away in an ambulance and brought to the ER would shut down her night of searching for Maisie. Her arm throbbed, but had it really all come down to quitting now?

As she held her phone, it began buzzing in her hand—the sheriff's department.

If nothing else, she thought, she could at least alert them to Jack's storage facility and tell them about Cyrus Sasani's attack.

She answered.

"Reece," came the voice of Chief Gomez, "I gotta tell you something. Landy issued a warrant for your ass and now everybody's out there searching for you."

"What!?" Reece gasped. "Now?"

"Yes, *now*. I'm only telling you this because…I'm pretty sure you're out looking for that double agent. If you have any leads, you need to tell me, because the CIA is about to make your life a living hell. If there's a chance to clear your name, it's now or never."

"How do you know I'm looking for Jack?"

"I already heard about all the shit you've been pulling these past few days. I'm no fool."

"Right. Sorry, Chief, I didn't mean—"

"All good," he interrupted. "I get it. Got anything?"

Reece told him about the storage facility and the events that had taken place.

Having the chief on her side was a positive; however, if she wanted to see this night through as planned, getting professional medical help appeared out of the question.

"I'll tell the guys some random witness called in," Gomez reassured her. "Hey, who knows, maybe we'll get all the proof we need to clear your name." Then: "Are you doing okay?"

Reece grimaced. "Yeah," she lied.

"Keep up the good work. Meanwhile, I'm gonna press Landy to search that guy Hawk's house. I heard what Shanahan had to say, and I don't give a damn what the bigwigs at the CIA think, I trust Shanahan's instincts."

Reece hung up with a mixture of relief and trepidation. Gomez believed her. But the rest of the department was out looking for her.

Off in the distance, there was a ranch she had seen from the storage facility. Surely the ranch would have medical supplies—if nothing else, for their animals.

Without any other good options, she slipped through the darkness towards the property.

*   *   *

Cyrus's lifeless body twitched slightly. Jack's hands still tightly gripped the gun he used—Reece Cannon's standard issue. He glanced around the storage facility searching for any signs of witnesses or surveillance cameras that might have caught him in the act.

Satisfied that he was alone and unrecorded, he began moving in the direction Reece had fled to, his confident stride exuding an air of superiority and arrogance like a man on top of his game.

He had punctured the tires on Reece's Jeep. She wasn't going anywhere.

His mind contemplated a thousand different scenarios. If his government believed his cover had been compromised, his life would be over. He needed to make sure they believed his American identity was still intact and infallible.

Jack's thoughts were also consumed with visions of glory and recognition. He imagined the adulation he would receive for completing his mission successfully.

At this moment, it seemed more and more likely that Reece Cannon would continue falling from grace, be convicted of multiple murders, and her story of him being a double agent would be construed as the ramblings of a desperate criminal.

Reece—the thought of her filled him with rage. Who did she think she was, going way above her duties as a lowly deputy?

Jessie was merely an afterthought; she would be dead soon enough, and by his own hand. Then he would portray her as a hysterical and irrational mess. He would say Hawk had been the one who had taped her to the chair, and that Lieutenant Shanahan hadn't known what he'd walked in to, and acted prematurely.

Cautiously, Jack approached Reece's Jeep, looking for her. She was nowhere to be seen.

Not far from the storage facility, amongst a smattering of nearby homes, he glimpsed a horse ranch about a quarter mile away, visible through a barren desert lot.

On the ground, he noticed the moon's shimmering reflection off of what appeared to be wet drops. He kneeled down, spotting a few blood drops here, and a few drops there—a trail that led in the ranch's direction.

Instead of heading directly to the property, he jogged farther down the road to his newly acquired vehicle, where Jessie's friend Maisie was bound and gagged inside. He would drive to the far side of the ranch to get a better view of the area, watching for any sign of Reece and what she may be up to.

As he slowly drove around the horse ranch, he continued scanning for any sign of his target, wondering what he would do when he found her. Would he also bind her, like Maisie, and then interrogate her for more information, or simply kill her on the spot?

He was the one with the power, the one in control.

Victory is within my grasp.

21

AFTER STEPPING FOOT on the ranch, Reece noticed a sign hanging on the front of the owner's house, illuminated by a flickering porch light.

VETERINARIAN

DR. ANNIE FLINT

(Go around back) →

It was now past midnight, and Reece hoped the woman was fast asleep. Reece's injured forearm throbbed with each step as she made her way around back, hoping to find bandages and supplies.

She tried the doorknob—unlocked. Upon easing the door open, the old hinges protested with a squeal. She stepped inside. The scent of lavender and cedar filled the air as she moved into a back office-looking area of the house.

The sound of footsteps approaching brought her heart to her throat. Anxiety surged as Reece braced for a confrontation with the homeowner.

A woman appeared in a nightgown, silver hair flowing over her shoulders. Confusion and fear traced the lines of her face.

Her eyes were drawn to Reece's bloody arm.

"What in tarnation are you doin' in my home?" she demanded, her voice a mix of caution and anger.

Reece displayed her gash, blood dripping from the tourniquet. "Annie Flint? I'm a sheriff's deputy, I swear to you. But I need your help. I saw your sign, and I—"

Annie's eyes widened as she took in the wound, her fingers gripping her nightgown tightly. "I can't help you. I don't have time for druggies and crooks."

"Listen, I don't have my badge on me, but I'm Reece Cannon, a sheriff's deputy for Pima County. Ten minutes. That's all I'm asking for."

Annie stared at Reece, her eyes lingering on the bloodied arm. "Then why ain't you goin' to the hospital?"

"It's complicated."

Annie hesitated, and they stood there staring at one another for a few moments, but eventually she relented with a reluctant expression. "Alright, I can spare you ten minutes. But only 'cuz I believe ya. If you were a druggie you would've just said you were a cop. That 'sheriff's deputy' thing is too specific."

"Thank you," Reece breathed out.

Annie eyed her with a suspicious smile. "You're on the run, ain't ya? That's why you don't have your badge."

Reece didn't have an angle. Or time. All she said was, "Yeah."

Annie laughed, and then motioned Reece to follow her to the other side of her home, to a room that looked like a doctor's office. She ordered Reece to sit in a chair while she removed supplies from a cabinet, including a needle and sutures.

Reece bit down on a cloth as Annie began to stitch up the gash, her hands steady.

"My late husband was a Vietnam vet, y'know," she said with the pride and nostalgia of a true cowgirl. "He would've been seventy-four this year."

"I'm sorry to hear he's gone," Reece mumbled with the cloth still in her mouth, her gaze dropping to the floor.

Annie chuckled softly. "Oh, that was a long time ago. He'd have gotten a kick out of you, though. Bursting into our home like some desperado on the run."

Reece managed a weak smile. "I guess that's not too far from the truth." Wanting to change the subject, she then nodded towards the stable and said, "Still ride the horses you have out there?"

"A couple. Mostly teach riding lessons on the weekends. You know, to high schoolers and such. My Scout out there in the stables, he's the friendliest fella you'd ever meet. Got this white patch on his flank that makes him stand out like a beacon in the night."

Reece clenched her jaw against the pain of the needle, her eyes meeting Annie's. "He sounds wonderful."

"He's a special one, alright," Annie said.

*   *   *

Captain Prestwood moved through the sheriff's department barking commands, surrounded by the tense voices of deputies. It was a scene of carefully controlled chaos, the hunt for Reece Cannon consuming his thoughts. Sheriff Landy had just come down hard on everyone, spittle flying from his lips as he yelled.

In the midst of the hustle and bustle, a voice sounded behind Prestwood. "Captain, I've got a new lead for you."

Prestwood spun around. "Chief Gomez,"—he said, immediately standing up a little straighter—"What is it?"

"Someone called in a report of gunshots fired at Tucson Self Storage, that facility at the edge of town. The caller said she was driving down the road when she heard the shots. You should send some guys to check it out. See what they find inside."

"You got it, Chief."

Just then, a deputy rapidly approached the two. "Captain, we've got a new lead!"

"Okay," Prestwood responded with a drawl, amazed two leads just came in at once. "Let's hear it."

"A guy just called in saying he and his buddy were out hunting scorpions near a place called Tucson Self Storage. In a desert lot—"

Gomez interrupted. "Hunting scorpions? What the hell?"

Prestwood answered without hesitation. "It's legal, and they fetch a pretty penny to the collectors. If you use a black light, they glow like a neon sign. My son used to do it too, when he was younger." He turned his attention back to the deputy. "Go on."

"The guy claims he heard gunshots, and then saw a woman, dressed in black, sneak onto the property of a nearby horse ranch. The guy's worried she's trying to steal some old lady's horses. And maybe worse, too."

Prestwood's jaw clenched, the gears of his mind grinding into action. "A woman?"

To Prestwood's surprise, Gomez scowled.

"Everything all right, Chief?" he asked.

"Fine," Gomez muttered.

Prestwood nodded, not sure what that look was about.

His voice boomed: "Well, what are we waiting for, deputy? Radio everyone; tell them to get out there, now!"

22

REECE GRITTED HER TEETH as the needle pierced her skin, her eyes closed against the pain. Annie was finishing up.

The sudden blare of sirens shattered Reece's meditation, and blue and red lights lit up the outside like a fireworks show. Sheriff's deputies swarmed the ranch like a pack of wolves.

Annie's hands froze mid-stitch. She glared out the window. "What the hell!?" she spat.

She backed away from Reece, her hands raised defensively. "I can't help you anymore. I can't be a part of this."

Reece's desperation fueled her resolve. She grabbed the nearby scissors and snipped the excess suture, spat the cloth out of her mouth, and then used it to wipe the blood from her arm. She grabbed the tape and gauze bandages from the table, and quickly, albeit sloppily, dressed her stitches, wrapping the tape around her entire arm like a rope.

She faced Annie, and said, "I understand. Just tell me how to get out of here without being seen."

Annie hesitated, seemingly torn. Finally, she pointed to a cabinet. "There's some ibuprofen and Tylenol in there. Take both. And there's a back door—not the one you came in, but on the other side of the house—leading to the horse barn. You'll have to be quiet, but if you go now, they ain't gonna see ya."

Reece grabbed the meds and swallowed the pills. With a nod of gratitude to Annie, she met the old woman's gaze, searching for her understanding. In her eyes, Reece found a quiet acceptance, and with it, a sense of redemption.

"Good luck, Reece," Annie whispered, her voice barely audible above the banging on her front door.

With a nod, Reece headed for the back, the reality of her fate sinking in.

As she moved through the quaint home, she noticed a table with some items on it, including a bag of carrots. She quickly grabbed a handful before stepping out the back door, just as the sound of police radios and Annie's defiant voice echoed from inside the home.

As the night closed in around Reece, she had one blaring thought: *Have I really become a fugitive?*

*   *   *

Jack leaned over the driver's seat, his eyes locking onto the bound figure of Maisie in the back of his rented Nissan Rogue. Besides gagging her, he had also placed a cloth bag over her head, for good measure.

He had ditched the Maserati, for now, not wanting any complications until he straightened everything out.

Unfortunately, the Rogue didn't have a trunk. However, so far, his threats at gunpoint had worked. He tapped her every so often with the barrel of his gun, too, for good measure.

Maisie hadn't moved an inch or made a peep. Fear can do that to a person.

A sinister smile played at the corners of his lips as he began to speak, the words spilling from him like poison-laced honey. "You know, Maisie, it's funny, isn't it? How Reece Cannon and those deputies, those so-called 'heroes,' just arrest one misguided guy at a time on some random escapade."

Maisie's terror was apparent in the muffled whimpers that escaped from within the bag.

Jack continued, his voice a low, menacing purr. "They're like little ants, scurrying around, never seeing the bigger picture. But me and what I do—it'll change the landscape of the entire world's power dynamics. They can't even begin to comprehend the scope of what I'm doing."

Maisie's body shuddered, her breath coming in panicked gasps, the gag in her mouth barely muffling her desperate pleas for mercy.

Jack watched the flickering of flashing lights at the horse ranch. Reece was there somewhere, hidden in the shadows.

He picked up the binoculars sitting on the passenger seat beside him and peered through.

"Ah, Maisie, it seems our little game is about to get a lot more interesting."

He murmured, almost to himself, "You see, Maisie, sometimes the most dangerous game is the one you don't even know you're playing."

*   *   *

The moonlight cast a white glow over Annie's horse ranch. The back of the property stretched out before Reece, the nearby stable doors offering a glimpse of the impressive beasts within. She stepped inside the stable, and the earthy scent of hay and horses enveloped her.

Her eyes immediately found Scout, the horse with the white marking Annie had mentioned. The idea of fleeing on horseback seemed ludicrous, but time was not on her side. She unlocked Scout's stable door, preparing to open it.

Reece's stitched up and bandaged arm still throbbed; her one good arm would have to be enough. Thoughts of Jack, Maisie, and her urgent need for vindication consumed her.

Fate, however, had a different script. From the darkness, a figure suddenly emerged, his size and features strangely akin to Cyrus Sasani. He charged without warning. Reece's heart skipped a beat, and she instinctually jumped backwards like a bolt of lightning.

Yet, before a single blow was dealt, the loud voices of deputies moving into the back area called out, issuing authoritative commands. The man froze, a look of contemplation on his face.

With no time to spare, Reece rolled under the stable door, kicked it open, and then launched herself from atop a hay bale, vaulting onto Scout's back, sans saddle. She could feel the powerful muscles of the horse beneath her, the promise of speed and freedom.

Urging Scout onward, they burst from the stable, jumped a small fence, and then raced into the desert while the deputies frantically began yelling and scrambling to close in on her.

The growl of a dirt bike's engine filled the air, and Reece's eyes darted back. The Cyrus Sasani doppelgänger tore out of the ranch, pursuing her.

Wind whipped through Reece's hair, and the thundering hooves of Scout blended with the bike's roar, drowning out the fading sound of the deputies on foot behind them.

The desert here was too lush for SUVs to follow. Depending on how far the pair traveled, it would take some time for the deputies to catch up—if they even could.

23

LIEUTENANT SHANAHAN entered Hawk Kelly's disheveled home, his gaze taking in the chaotic scene before him. The smell of stale takeout wafted through the air, while the remnants of Hawk's last meal—an empty KFC bucket—sat dejectedly on the couch.

Shanahan wrinkled his nose at the piles of food wrappers strewn haphazardly around the room. There were stacks of unopened mail on the coffee table, and a sink full of dirty dishes. The floors needed a good mopping too.

FBI agents and a few CIA operatives milled about, rifling through Hawk's thrown-about belongings with an air of urgency. They were searching for evidence that would confirm the dead man's double life—there was a lot of mess to sift through—yet their efforts had so far been fruitless. Shanahan and Reece's testimonies were the only clues hinting at Hawk's duplicity.

As Shanahan observed the frenzied activity, he sought the overlooked details that might elude less perceptive minds. "Excuse me," he murmured as he picked his way through the room, careful not to disturb any potential evidence.

His attention was drawn to a solitary houseplant in the kitchen corner, its presence an incongruous detail amidst the disarray. Resting on a small pedestal, the plant seemed lonely, its pot bearing traces of spilled soil.

Lifting the plant gently, Shanahan examined the pot and discovered it was heavier than anticipated. Turning it sideways, he revealed a concealed compartment at the bottom. Inside, he found a single key.

With anticipation mounting, Shanahan searched for a lock that might match the key. He noticed an antique floor lamp in the living room, its base adorned with intricate carvings. One particular carving caught his attention: a small, nearly imperceptible keyhole.

Inserting the key into the keyhole, Shanahan turned it, and the lamp's base emitted a faint click. Twisting the base, he unveiled another hidden compartment containing a small, round object—a battery-operated, remote-controlled device.

Shanahan examined the device, noting that it had a single button. Pressing it, he scanned the room to see if anything changed. Nothing seemed to have happened.

He proceeded to search the house. In the master bedroom, his keen eyes detected a faint vertical fissure in the crown molding. He grabbed a chair, climbed onto it, and pushed the crown molding panel aside, revealing yet another hidden compartment.

Reaching inside, Shanahan grasped a small electronic device, removing it. It appeared custom-made—some sort of hybrid between a walkie-talkie and an old Blackberry phone.

With the device in hand, Shanahan descended from the chair. "Gentlemen," he announced to the gathering cluster of agents, "Perhaps this is what we've been looking for."

24

SCOUT'S HOOVES POUNDED against the dirt, the brush and cacti blurring by as the horse galloped at a breakneck speed. On the dirt bike behind, her pursuer accelerated closer, until he finally pulled up alongside the horse.

Reece saw that in the man's hand was a gun, and he was attempting to level it straight at her.

With her injured arm, Reece fumbled in her pocket and pulled out a few carrots. She hurled them in his direction, forcing him to dodge the projectiles. It was almost amusing; if he only knew they were merely carrots.

As he swerved, Reece took advantage of his momentary distraction and steered Scout away in a zigzag pattern. A second later, he fired a shot.

The bullet whistled past Reece.

She reached for her Glock, but the only way she was going to effectively use it was with her good arm, which meant she had to let go of her grip on the horse's mane.

She did, then firing a return shot, but that shot scared Scout and he jumped, knocking Reece sideways. She wildly reached for the horse's mane—and dropped her gun in the process. Scout then haphazardly darted a half dozen yards away before she resumed control of the animal.

The dirt bike had whipped around and was now right on Reece again. The man fired again, this time aimed at Scout.

From prior experience, Reece knew that horses move off, or away, from pressure in a turn. So, thinking quickly, she dug the heel of her left shoe into the horse, spurring a sudden right turn, narrowly avoiding the bullet that would have struck the animal.

Dirt spewed from the spinning tires as the bike did a 90° turn and closed in again. On a hunch, Reece turned Scout to directly face the dirt bike, and then called out, "Up!" while leaning backwards, clenching her thighs and holding on for dear life. The horse reared up and brought its front legs down on the bike's handlebars. The impact immediately sent the bike to the ground in a plume of dust, the man's body tumbling over the dirt.

Jack watched from a distance as Reece fought the man. Jack knew who he was—Darius Sasani, Cyrus's twin brother.

A reluctant smirk tugged at the corner of Jack's lips. "Do you see, Maisie?" he sneered, gesturing towards the distant figures locked in combat, even though she couldn't see anything from inside the bag.

"Oh, you can't see?" He reached back and tapped her head with his gun again, eliciting a whimper from the woman.

"Looks like our dear friend Reece is quite the fighter. Who would've thought?" His voice dripped with sarcastic disdain.

Jack mulled over his next move, the possibilities unfurling like an intricate spiderweb. Should he confront Reece or Darius next? Or, perhaps, he could let them destroy each other, leaving him free to finish off Maisie, and then get back to Jessie and his plan to make her death look like a suicide. He chuckled at that thought.

His ego swelled like a balloon about to burst, inflated by the perverse thrill of holding another's fate in his hands. He was the puppet master, the one who controlled every move and action.

And yet, as he pondered his next move, the dirt bike went down, sending Darius sprawling. A flicker of doubt gnawed at the edge of his mind.

For a brief moment the veneer of his confidence slipped. But, as quickly as it had disappeared, it returned.

"Oh, Maisie," he sighed, almost wistfully, "let's see how this little game plays out, shall we?"

* * *

Reece guided Scout to a temporary halt as the faint breeze whispered an eerie lament through the night. Exhausted and aching, the odds were stacked against her and she knew it.

She scanned the area where her gun had fallen but didn't see it. With her non-existent arsenal, her chances of victory seemed thin.

She briefly thought of those movies where the hero or heroine loaded up on guns and ammo, and then went careening after the bad guys, taking armies down with limitless bullets.

Yeah, that wasn't her—even with her quick reflexes and younger-days street-fighting experience. Right now, it was all she could do to maintain enough confidence to keep going.

The insistent buzz of her phone snapped her back to reality. Retrieving it from her pocket, she saw the same strange number from earlier in the night—now for the third time. Desperately in need of support, this time, hope, that fragile and fleeting thing, won out.

Inhaling deeply, she answered.

"Reece!" Shanahan's voice came through, resolute and steady. "I believe in you. I've got your back."

These were the first words out of his mouth. They required no explanation on her part, and they flowed over her, soothing her frayed nerves and reigniting her self-confidence.

"Shan," she said with relief.

He pressed on, "I found something at Hawk's house. But where are you? I can't help if I'm not there."

The moment of respite was abruptly shattered by the sound of pounding footsteps rapidly closing in. Reece's assailant, illuminated in the moon's light, raised his gun and aimed it straight at her.

25

REECE RELEASED HER GRASP on the phone,
dropping it to the powdery dirt. But the line remained
open.

The weight of her decisions flashed through her
mind. Thoughts of Maisie, abducted and vulnerable,
and Jessie, deluded by Jack, rippled through her.

The desert night had become Reece's
battleground; she had no choice but to fight—or die.

As the man aimed his weapon, Reece leapt from
her horse, dodging the bullet by a hair's breadth. She
slapped Scout's rump, and dove for refuge behind a
cluster of boulders on the uneven terrain. Scout
galloped away, disappearing into the shadows of a
nearby wash.

"Reece! Are you there? What's happening?"
Shanahan's voice could be heard over the phone's little
speaker, though faint, as he bore witness to the sounds
of the unfolding confrontation.

"You're a mere pawn in a much larger game," the
man taunted at Reece. "Do you honestly think you can
make a difference?"

Shanahan's voice, urgent and commanding, carried over the phone. "Reece, use anything you can to defend yourself! You're resourceful!"

From behind the boulders, Reece heard the man sneer. "Got yourself a cheerleader, do you?"

Reece's thoughts burned bright and hot, moving from Maisie and Jessie to the broader implications of her actions. The flawed, yet indispensable systems that shaped her world—American freedoms, the Pima County Sheriff's Department, the criminal justice system—it all deserved to be upheld and honored, even in their imperfection. She was a part of something bigger, something worth fighting for.

If it wasn't for every piece of its existence, she wouldn't have been there for Jessie in the first place with a badge and a purpose.

Then Reece got a crazy idea. With practiced ease, she removed her bra while leaving her shirt on. Scooping up a handful of sizeable rocks, she filled one of the cups and tied it shut, crafting an impromptu weapon—a bra sling.

The man's voice rang out again. "But if you're dead set on playing hero, then let's see what you've got."

Still crouched behind the boulders, Reece shouted, "I'm right here, ready and waiting!"

The man's footsteps grew louder as he approached the spot where Reece hid. At the last possible second, she sprang up, meeting him head-on. The bra sling sliced through the air, hurtling towards the man with astonishing speed.

Thwack!

The weapon, a testament to her resourcefulness, struck his midsection with a cracking force. Reece then kicked out, knocking the gun from his hand the way Jack had done to her earlier in Jessie's backyard.

The man reeled back, his eyes narrowing, glancing between the gun that landed in a thick patch of prickly pear, and Reece. For a moment he stood still, as if contemplating his next move. His eyes were cold and calculated, a predator sizing up its prey.

"I'm going to enjoy this, girl!" he spat, his voice laced with venom. He lunged at Reece, fists clenched and face contorted.

Reece dodged, her body moving with a fluidity that seemed to defy gravity as she swung the bra sling at him again. He dodged to the side, but then lunged again, successfully grabbing the bra sling while Reece recovered from the momentum of the rotation. A brief tug-of-war ensued, ending with the rocks tumbling from the bra.

The man pulled out a knife, its blade glinting under the pale light. Reece shivered, sensing the gash in her arm. She scanned the area for anything to use as a weapon.

Her eyes settled on a broken shovel handle lying nearby, and she dove for it just as the man lunged with his knife.

As he came at her again, Reece parried the strike with the handle, then jabbed it towards the man's chest. He dodged, but that gave Reece a chance to spring to her feet.

He lunged again, his blade whooshing through the air. Reece sidestepped the attack and countered with a vicious swing of the handle, catching the man on the side of the head.

He stumbled back, dazed. Reece seized the opportunity, smashing the handle against his wrist, causing him to drop the knife. But he kicked her in the side, knocking her off balance.

The man's clothes had been torn and stained with sweat and dirt, while Reece's own attire, tattered, bloody and worn, spoke to the ferocity of their determination.

Amidst the clash of wills, Shanahan's coffee mug from the break room flashed through her mind, and she remembered Thucydides' words: *The secret of happiness is freedom, and the secret of freedom is courage.* The words reverberated in her soul like a beacon of sheer doggedness.

This fight was a testament to the freedom she so desperately sought. In this moment, she was both the unstoppable force and the immovable object, a living embodiment of the indomitable spirit of humanity.

*   *   *

Looking through the binoculars, Jack's eyes were locked on the fierce battle between Reece Cannon and Darius Sasani. He raised an eyebrow, caught off guard by the sight of Reece wielding her makeshift bra sling.

As Jack observed the violent dance between Darius and Reece, he found himself strangely captivated. From the sounds of the PCSD vehicle's sirens and the flashing lights, to the battle he watched, there was no denying the night air was charged with electricity.

But as the sheriff's SUVs moved closer, beginning to encircle the area, he decided it was time to find a better location to park the vehicle.

As he drove away, Jack was content to let the chips fall where they may. If Darius were to emerge victorious, so be it. And if Reece somehow managed to triumph over her formidable opponent, well, that would be a sight to behold.

Regardless, he wasn't going far.

26

DARIUS SASANI had been confident that he would emerge victorious, that this would be just another battle to add to his ever-growing list of conquests. But now he stood unsteady, his wrist broken and his ribs cracked.

The battle resumed with renewed intensity, the desert bearing witness to their struggle. Reece lunged for his lost knife, grabbing it from the ground and using it to drive him back, its point burying deep into his shoulder. He howled in pain, a primal sound escaping from his lips, surprising even him.

As Darius faltered, he saw Reece reach for a discarded hubcap, its metal surface gleaming beneath the moon's watchful gaze. It became a makeshift shield as she charged, blocking his attacks before she delivered a sweeping kick to the side of his knee. He heard a crack and felt searing pain. He crumpled.

Then, Darius's eyes locked onto an unexpected interloper—a Diamondback Rattlesnake, coiled and ready to strike. The warning rattle was a hit to his senses, and in that heartbeat of time, he was forced to make a split-second decision.

He scrambled away from the venomous predator, narrowly evading its fangs, his broken knee screaming in agony. Darius had lunged sideways and now ended up flat on his stomach—giving Reece an opening.

"It looks like the snake's got better aim than you," she quipped.

Darius felt Reece's knee stab into his spine, and his bleeding shoulder burned with pain as the woman grabbed his hands behind him, zip tying them together.

Darius gritted his teeth, a bitter laugh escaping his lips as he pondered the cruel twist of fate that had brought him to this place. How had he ended up here, bested by a mere woman in a foreign land? He had left a good life in Iran for his government's cause, but now he found himself wondering if it had all been worth it.

As he tried to roll over, to stand and fight, a sense of overwhelming misfortune washed over him. He thought back to his homeland and the family he had left behind, wondering if his ill-fated journey to this godforsaken desert had sealed his fate, just like his brother's.

*   *   *

After zip tying Darius's hands, he still struggled, attempting to roll over. Reece seized the hubcap and brought it crashing down onto his face, sending him back to the dirt. Grabbing another zip tie, she swiftly secured his ankles, neutralizing any further threat he might pose.

When the dust settled, she registered wetness on her injured arm—some of her stitches must've ripped open and blood soaked her bandages.

Good thing the pain meds kicked in. Or, she thought, *maybe it's just the adrenaline.*

Reece stood and glanced around. The deputies who had been at the ranch were making noise in the distance, calling to each other as they traversed on foot. There had to be a dozen of them out there, moving cautiously towards them.

Reece kneeled beside the defeated man. "Where's Jack?" she demanded.

"I don't know," Darius spat.

"You're Cyrus Sasani's brother, aren't you?"

"Was it you?" he asked, with an odd combo of snarky and melancholy.

The inflection in his voice, the way he said it—it could only mean one thing.

"I just saw him alive, minutes ago," Reece countered.

"Then you were a minute too soon." Imitating Reece in a more sarcastic tone, he continued, "I just saw him *dead,* minutes ago."

Then he began murmuring an apology to his country under his breath. But his words went unheard, save for Reece and the starry expanse above.

Reece stood to leave. The other deputies would find this man soon enough—and she needed to get out of there before they found *her*.

He glanced sideways at Reece as she took a step back, a blend of awe and resentment in his eyes. "I was supposed to kill Jamshid and you both," he admitted.

"Well, you've clearly failed on both counts."

She paused, again recalling Thucydides' words: *...the secret of freedom is courage.*

But wasn't this man also courageous, simply from a different perspective, in his own beliefs?

No, Reece thought, *he is visibly full of anger and rage. There is a vulnerability to courage. Rage is the refusal to feel vulnerability.*

As she pondered these thoughts, she snatched up her dropped phone from earlier, its screen cracked but still functional. "Shanahan, did you hear all that?"

"I heard everything," Shanahan replied, concern lacing his voice. "Are you okay?"

"Okay enough."

"That sounded like a damn good fight." Then: "It's all over the radio that you unlawfully entered a vet's home office for medical attention. Are you still near that ranch?"

"Pretty close, relatively. There's a wash north of the place. If you follow the wash east, that's where I am now, on the southern edge—but not where I'm going to be," Reece informed him, her voice steady. "The other deputies will be here soon. Let them know his last name may be Sasani. But I don't know the first."

"Reece, you need to tell me where you're going. You can't do this alone, rookie. Where is Maisie?—do you know?"

"Not yet, but I think Jack is following me. I was attacked at Tucson Self Storage by a man who called himself Cyrus Sasani, and I retreated. According to his brother here, he's now dead. I'm betting it was Jack. And the difference in possible timeframes between when I saw Cyrus alive and his brother seeing him dead could only be minutes. I'm betting he'll come to me. I'm going to keep heading east with the wash."

"I'll come find you. I'm already on my way. And I found a device at Hawk's. Landy hasn't dropped your warrant yet, but I'm betting there's proof on the device that will indicate what he was really up to. Don't do anything stupid in the meantime, got it?"

"I kinda think that already happened."

She ended the call and then jogged to the wash, ducking down into it. Time was of the essence. And if Jack wanted her, this would be the time and the place for a confrontation.

*　*　*

Riding passenger in the sheriff's SUV, Shanahan thought about his high school friend turned unorthodox rookie—Reece Cannon. What the hell happened to her during the last few years when she was gone?

This woman not only managed to survive the vicissitude of being hunted, but even flipped it to become the hunter? He was curious to understand what was driving her, what had changed her since he'd last seen her in high school.

The more he pondered, the more absurd it even appeared that Reece had opted to work in law enforcement. She had always been the rebellious type, doing things just because she wasn't supposed to.

As the SUV sped down the roads, rookie Ethan Wilson, still wet behind the ears, gripped the steering wheel beside him.

Shanahan believed he could trust Ethan; underneath the 'bro' personality, Shanahan saw a capable and genuine man.

The headlights pierced the darkness as they drew closer to the wash Reece had indicated. Shanahan braced for the confrontation that lay ahead. He knew courage would determine this night's fate—courage, and the unbreakable will to fight for what was right.

27

REECE FOLLOWED the dry wash east, watching its ridge for any sign of movement. Her gaze lingered on a swaying Palo Verde tree, dancing under the moonlight. She wasn't completely in the middle of nowhere; in this area, older homes dotted the north side of the wash, some of the backyards even butting up against it.

Clutching the last remaining carrot, Reece called for Scout as she moved, her mind replaying the earlier altercation with her attacker. The memory of hurling carrots at him brought a fleeting, wry smile to her lips—even though her heart felt like it was beating as fast as a hummingbird's wings. She assumed Jack was following her, maybe even watching her right now.

A familiar silhouette appeared not far off—Scout, standing tall and proud. Reece slowly approached the horse—a "special one" indeed, as Annie Flint had described him. She offered him the carrot, her fingers brushing his velvety muzzle as he snatched up the treat, his eyes gleaming with recognition.

For a moment, time seemed to stand still as Reece and Scout shared a tender exchange. She stroked his mane, her touch gentle but firm, and she whispered kind words into his ear.

The Sonoran Desert surrounded them, a place that defied the notion of deserts being barren and lifeless. But tonight, the desert held darker secrets. The wind seemed to howl a warning, rustling the mesquite branches.

Reece's gut instincts, that innate sense that guided her and led her to trust or avoid certain individuals, flared to life. She strained to hear any telltale sounds, her eyes searching the darkness for any hint of danger.

As if on cue, the moon emerged from behind a shroud of clouds. It was under this ghostly illumination that Reece's gaze fell upon the menacing figure of Jack, looming on higher ground. Seemingly unaware of her presence, he surveyed the landscape with an air of predatory intent.

Jack's elevated position afforded him a bird's-eye view of the wash, a strategic advantage that left him poised for an attack. In his grip, a gun gleamed.

Reece studied him. No one would know simply by looking at him that Jack was a man who remained indifferent, or even satisfied, at the bloodshed of others. He was handsome, his jawline set like a prince. His dimpled smile seemingly warm.

Despite his ignorance of her exact location, the air seemed to crackle with tension as Jack called out, "I didn't bother fighting you before, because I thought Darius would take care of you. Clearly, he was incompetent."

His declaration hung heavy in the air, his voice dripping with arrogance and disdain.

"Come out now, Reece Cannon, and I promise you a swift, merciful death," he taunted, the cruel satisfaction in his voice evident. "Show yourself!"

Crouched near Scout, her heart pounding like a drumbeat of war, Reece's eyes fell upon an object half-buried in the sand—a length of rope, its frayed ends ravaged by time.

I hope it still has some strength left to it.

Soon the clouds passed in front of the moon again, rendering the landscape darkened once again.

She seized the rope, testing its durability with a firm tug. To her relief, it held fast. With swift, precise movements, she tethered Scout to a nearby tree trunk.

*   *   *

Jack walked the wash's edge, scanning for movement while the moon shone, and listening when it became hidden.

His thoughts were calculated. It was always possible Reece had backup on the way—perhaps that impersonator from earlier, Lieutenant Shanahan.

That's why he remained out in the open. He wanted to draw Reece out, to have her give away her hiding spot by mistakenly believing she might have the upper hand. And if Shanahan was near, he would assuredly do the same.

Finally, he heard movement in the bushes below, near a tree.

There she is.

28

REECE HEARD JACK'S FOOTFALLS; he was making his way directly towards her. She realized he must've heard her tether Scout to the tree.

Taking a deep breath, she readied herself for what was to come next. She remained hidden in the shadows, at the crossroads of a story near its end, a tale of lies and redemption.

The moon reappeared, and with it, enough light to see a dozen or so feet away. Surveying the landscape around her, Reece's eyes locked onto a cholla cactus—the deceptive teddy bear cholla, with its needle-like spines that punished the unwary, promising that a brush with its arms would result in hours of painstaking work as one used tweezers to extract the countless barbs latched onto their flesh.

Her plan set, Reece hurled a rock at the cholla, making a *thunk* sound as it smacked against it. Jack's gun thundered in response, bullets ripping through the air. And then, once again, only the sound of the light breeze remained. After a moment, Jack slunk closer, headed towards the cholla.

Another patchwork of clouds moved over the moon, blocking its glow yet again. Reece could barely see two feet in front of her now. The clouds were getting thicker and coming in larger patches, and the breeze suddenly kicked up too.

This was her chance.

Reece burst from the shadows using her body as a weapon. She rammed into Jack, seeking to propel him into the treacherous embrace of the cholla. He stumbled, the cactus's spines latching and sinking into his left arm, but the attack wasn't as devastating as Reece had hoped. With a muscled frame, he was substantially heavier than Reece. Instead of knocking him down and into it, Jack's brush with the cholla only served to fuel his rage.

Growling like a wounded animal, Jack lashed out, his fists cutting through the air like blades. But his frenzied swings found only empty space, his target elusive. Reece had darted back into the shadows before he was able to see where she had gone.

Seemingly undeterred, he barked at Reece: "If anything you could do actually mattered, I would have already figured out how to overcome it. Whatever you think you can do, you can't."

His words struck a nerve. What *was* she going to do, besides doing everything possible to not trip over anything and make more noise? She huddled near Scout, listening as the sound of Jack's steps moved closer to them.

"No gun, though, huh?" he called out with a snicker.

As Jack approached, Reece's hand closed around a small, smooth rock—seemingly insignificant, yet holding within its humble form the potential for salvation. Or, perhaps, disaster. A plan formed in her mind, a last-ditch effort to turn the tide of this deadly confrontation.

As Jack closed the gap, Reece's grip on the rock tightened, her breath held in a vice-like restraint, waiting for him to be in the perfect spot.

The breeze died down, leaving the air still.

Every step Jack took, every beat of her heart, brought her closer to the decisive moment.

A dance with fate.

With the culmination of her plan drawing near, Reece held the rock firmly within her grasp, poised to be unleashed.

She didn't dare even breathe. The silence would amplify any breath.

Scout, her faithful horse, was tied securely to the gnarled trunk of a mesquite tree only a few feet away. He was being still; perhaps he was even sleeping. Perfect.

As Jack moved closer, Reece thought about justice.

Justice is about enforcing common decency. Justice is about being held accountable. Justice is about corrective action. Justice is about moving forward with a plan for peace. And Reece wanted all of that for Jessie, for Maisie, for Pima County—for the entirety of this country, coast to coast with every little town between—and also, for herself.

Each step of Jack's was like the move of a chess piece, as he, seemingly unbeknownst to him, moved closer and closer to Scout—Reece's checkmate—the horse's still silhouette an agonizing promise.

One more step later, he finally moved into position.

Reece hurled the rock straight at Jack. She didn't throw it hard; she threw it accurately. The rock hit him square in the chest. With lightning-fast reaction speed, he spun in the direction of Reece, crunching the debris on the ground and making noise, beginning to raise his gun in her direction.

But the sudden movement caught Scout off-guard, and the horse, driven by instinct and fear, unleashed a powerful straight-back kick. One of Scout's hooves collided with Jack's upper thigh, the sound of bone and muscle crunching like a sledgehammer on a watermelon. Jack hurtled backward, thumping on the desert ground.

His body, once a finely tuned instrument of death, was now reduced to a crumpled heap in the parched dirt.

Reece cautiously approached the fallen figure. As she drew nearer, the full extent of Jack's incapacitation became apparent. The once-proud killer was now a shattered vessel. The horse's kick had distorted his leg, and blood stained his pants and shirt.

He wretched sideways, coughing up blood. The once-imposing figure, now rendered pitiful and weak, writhed in agony, his breaths coming in shallow gasps. His gun lay a few feet away from his grasp. Reece grabbed it.

The desert wind began whispering through the air, playfully toying with the ragged strands of his hair. The shadows cast by the moonlight danced across his face, forming a grotesque mask accentuating the anguish that contorted his features.

Like a marionette with its strings severed, Jack seemed a mere caricature of what he had once been.

Reece's eyes locked onto the pitiful figure. Was it possible to feel compassion for a creature so consumed by darkness?

29

AS THE CLOUDS reopened for the moon to peek through, its light returning to the landscape, Reece looked up to see figure materialize from the blackness, the moonlight glinting off his badge, revealing him to be none other than Lieutenant Shanahan. His eyes swept across the scene before him, taking in the unexpected triumph that had played out.

Reece's uneasiness melted at the sight of her long-time friend and mentor. Shanahan strode towards the pair, the wind ruffling the collar of his khaki-colored uniform shirt.

"Well, Reece, it looks like I missed all the fun."

Reece couldn't help but let out a breathy, incredulous laugh. A release of some serious tension.

Ethan appeared behind Shanahan, coming into the wash from a different angle. "Did you actually take him out!? I'm, like, majorly impressed."

"Ethan? You're here too?"

"Wouldn't have missed it…er, at least, tried not to."

Shanahan crouched down beside Jack, his gaze hardening as he assessed the damage inflicted by Reece and Scout. "You did a number on him, that's for sure," he remarked. "Not many people can say they went toe-to-toe with a killer—or three—and lived to tell the tale."

"It's not over yet," Reece answered. Then she turned to Jack. "Where's Maisie?" she demanded.

"Piss off," he grumbled back.

*　　*　　*

Reece, Shanahan, and Ethan ventured into the old neighborhood north of the wash, their eyes scanning the quiet streets for any sign of his black Maserati. The only sounds they heard were the hum of cicadas.

It was Ethan who discovered the Nissan Rogue. It had been parked behind a large dumpster next to a house that appeared to be in the process of being remodeled.

Reece and Shanahan came running over as Ethan snatched a large rock from the ground and smashed it through the driver's side window, then reaching in and hitting the unlock button.

Reece flung open the rear door to reveal the horror that had been hidden inside. Maisie lay on the floor, her body bound with a dark-colored bag over her head.

Shanahan helped her to her feet while Reece ripped the bag off, revealing her mouth gagged, and her eyes wide and glassy with terror. The sight of this woman, so vulnerable and helpless, sent a wave of righteous fury coursing through Reece's veins.

With trembling hands, Reece and Shanahan worked quickly to free Maisie from her cruel restraints. As the last of the bindings fell away, Maisie crumpled into Reece's arms.

The floodgates of emotion burst open, and tears cascaded down Maisie's cheeks, her body wracked with sobs. She clung to Reece, her fingers digging into Reece's shoulders as if to anchor herself to a world that had suddenly become terrifying and unfamiliar. Her breath came in chokes, each stuttered inhalation a testament to the horrors she had endured.

Reece held her, her own eyes glistening with unshed tears as Shanahan's eyes met them.

"Hey," Ethan called out, removing something from the car. "Is this important?"

In his hand was the iPhone lookalike.

30

THURSDAY ENDED but Reece didn't really sleep. Nightmares came. Faces crumbled.

After finding Maisie, Reece took a trip to the emergency room to re-stitch her arm properly. Then she had been at the station for hours, answering questions fired at her from Captain Prestwood, Chief Gomez, and Sheriff Landy, sometimes all at once—though it was obvious Gomez had been on her side from the get-go.

Apparently, during her interrogation, the FBI's forensics team finally cracked the code into the device Shanahan had found at Hawk's, and they—lo and behold— discovered top-secret CIA documents and evidence tying him to Saudi Arabia. Turns out his real name was Al Haqq Khan, and he was a foreign intelligence agent too. Go figure.

On top of that, Jack's fake iPhone provided proof of who he was.

Also, Shanahan, Jessie, and Maisie's testimonies, and Shanahan's recording of Reece's fight with Darius Sasani, along with his interrogation, unsurprisingly and drastically caused the tide to turn, and Reece's arrest warrant was dropped.

While that was all a victory, Reece's nerves were still completely shot.

When she finally got home, she might've dozed off for a couple early-morning hours, but even then, she kept waking up from unpredictable surges of adrenaline.

Friday morning's sun rose, Reece's teeth somehow got brushed, and she found herself driving back to the station.

She forgot to make coffee.

How does someone forget to make coffee? Could she ask Sheriff Landy for a couple days off? Or would that be pushing her luck?

And then she remembered.

Ugh. I might not be under arrest, but Landy never mentioned anything about my continued employment.

When she arrived to the station, to Reece's surprise, Shanahan had bagels and coffee waiting for her. Ethan—who also looked wrecked—had already eaten two.

But not Shanahan. Shanahan looked fine.

"How the heck are you even awake?" she asked him.

"Are you kidding? I passed out as soon as my head hit the pillow. Not my first rodeo, Reece. How's your arm?"

"Hurts. But it'll be okay."

"FYI, Landy just sent us emails. He wants to see us in his office—now."

"I like this gig, Shanahan. And things finally just got interesting. But I overstepped."

"You saved a beautiful woman's life. And her friend's too. And maybe even mine. I'll back you up, like I said before. And I still can't comprehend how the hell everything all worked out."

"A '*beautiful*' woman? Are you referring to Jessie?—do you stalk victims often?" Reece teased.

"Shut it, rookie. Anyway, let's get this over with. I'll bring Landy coffee and a bagel. Maybe that'll smooth his feathers a little."

The door to Landy's office was closed. Reece knocked. Four raps. As she knocked, she was reminded of the song, or rather, the piece of music she used to listen to back in chess club before a championship match.

Beethoven's Fifth Symphony. *Dun, dun, dun, duumm; dun, dun, dun, duumm.* Beethoven had said it represented 'fate knocking at the door.'

That was exactly how it felt.

Fate.

"Get in here," came the response from the other side of the door.

Being summoned to Sheriff Landy's desk generally meant not-so-good things, as she was well aware.

Landy spoke. "Executive Director David Pomeroy at the CIA called back this morning and congratulated me on my excellent department. Apparently, you two accomplished something just short of a miracle. An Iranian spy and a Saudi Arabian spy, in the same office, taken down the same night. Spies are crawling around like spiders and you both stepped on them."

Shanahan took a small step backwards. "Actually, sir, I can't take much credit. Reece had the plan, took out Al Haqq, fought the Sasani brothers—"

Landy interrupted. "I don't want to hear another word like that. As far as the media, America, and the whole entire world is concerned, you gave the orders, Shanahan, and Reece just came through. Promotions are coming up—for *both* of you—but I can't let every rookie in here thinking they can go rogue and bend the rules like that, or there'll be chaos and people will get hurt."

Landy looked directly at Reece. "I hope you understand."

"I still work here?"

"No more stunts, Reece."

"Of course, sir, I understand completely. Thank you, sir."

"Here." Shanahan handed over the bagel and coffee.

Landy finally cracked a smile. "Now that's more like it." He took a sip and sat back in his leather chair. "I think you two work well together. You know each other or something?"

"We went to the same high school," Shanahan replied.

"Well, I like it. I think you guys have something going. Make me proud. Now get outta here before I change my mind."

The deputies left, gently closed the door behind them, and then high fived like the old times.

"So, where're you headed, Reece?"

"Back to my desk."

"No, I mean in life. What's on your agenda?"

Reece's prior few years ran through her mind. Someday she'd tell Shanahan everything that happened to her while living in Los Angeles. But not right this second.

After her time in the big city, she wasn't in a hurry to make any major plans or settle down. This new career was just beginning, and she'd see it through.

Reece joked, "Take down the bad guys. Destroy villainous lives. When I have a free second, maybe dye my hair again. Normal girl stuff."

Shanahan chuckled. "I missed that attitude. Nice to have you around again." Then: "What color?"

"The color of fire."

Ethan walked over, interrupting Shanahan's look of concern.

"Which kind of bagel do you brotholomews like best? I don't want to eat your favs and there's only a few left." Ethan held a half-empty box with a plastic knife already covered in cream cheese.

Shanahan laughed. "You're literally my hero. How much can you fit in there?"

"Enough to power the gym sessions." Ethan flexed like a bodybuilding model on a magazine cover, his hands still comically full of bagels and cream cheese. "I just burn through it."

"Ethan, you look like a jackass." Reece gave him a look. "But I like you. I have a feeling we're all going to work well together."

"Honestly, Reece, if you pull any more of those magic ninja moves you pulled last night, I'm gonna be working for *you* in no time—and gladly. You played the detective part well." Ethan nodded to Shanahan. "And you too, bro. Congrats."

Reece smiled.

Even though Reece was sleep deprived and a bit on edge, she was starting to feel pretty damn good. Finally.

After a little more chitchat, Ethan walked off with two more bagels. Reece planned to return to her desk, too, but before she did, she lingered for a moment with Shanahan.

"Ah, yes?" Shanahan asked.

"You asked me what I have planned for the future."

"You gonna be serious with me now?"

"I'm gonna find out why you always smell like peppermint."

"I like mints, okay?" Shanahan's face colored.

Reece punched his shoulder and walked away, thinking to herself.

Sure you do.

Epilogue
FIVE MONTHS LATER

REECE AND SHANAHAN headed to lunch on an easygoing Thursday afternoon. Reece's promotion to detective was finally official, and they were celebrating.

They decided on a local place called Zin Burger. Reece couldn't get enough of their zucchini fries, and Shanahan liked their signature burger. Win-win.

When they pulled open the entrance doors, two women walked out. One of them was a tan woman with dark hair, who bumped right into them.

"Oh, sorry…" she began, before realizing who she bumped into.

"Jessie," Shanahan whispered.

Jessie stood there, staring like a star-struck fan next to Maisie. They both looked happy and well.

"It's you," Jessie whispered back.

Reece traded a few kind words with Maisie while Shanahan remained still, gazing awkwardly at Jessie before mumbling, "I guess I should, um, go." His voice conveyed very little conviction regarding leaving.

"Wait. Do you…do you come here a lot?" Jessie flipped her hair.

Shanahan's face lit up like he'd just won the lottery. "Yes! I mean…not really. Sometimes. I'm technically on duty right now, so…"

"So you're not supposed to ask for a woman's number when on duty?"

"That's probably frowned upon. But if you'd like, I can give you my card?"

"Too formal." Jessie tilted her head slightly. "Math, right?"

"Right," Shanahan said softly.

"See if you can remember this." Jessie recited her number as fast as she could, obviously enjoying herself.

"No problem."

"I hope so," she said.

"Five-two-zero…" Shanahan spit it out, exact of course, even faster than she'd recited it.

"Call me!" Jessie pranced off.

A few minutes later, after being sat at a table and passing a few jokes back and forth, Reece had the most delicious zucchini fries Zin Burger had ever made.

Shanahan acted like a giddy schoolboy.

Reece was now a detective.

Thursdays were good.

THE END

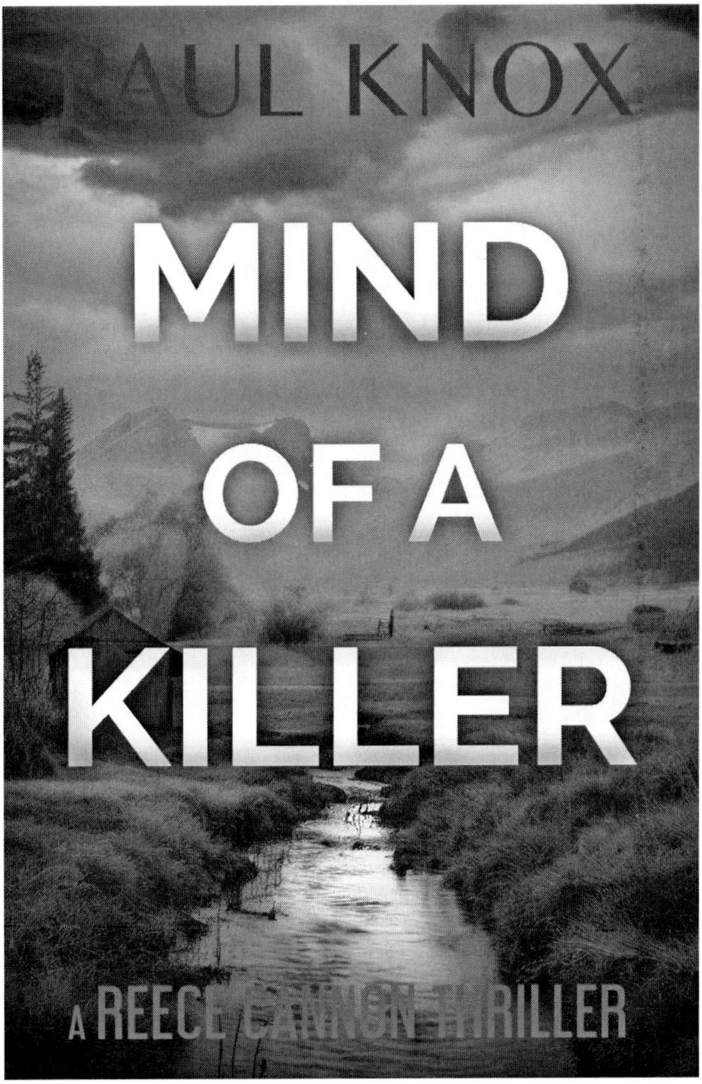
PAUL KNOX
MIND
OF A
KILLER
A REECE CANNON THRILLER

PREVIEW: MIND OF A KILLER

A Reece Cannon Thriller: Volume 2

PAUL KNOX

Prologue

DETECTIVE REECE CANNON stumbled out of the building, her body wracked with pain. Blood seeped through her fingers, and the world around her seemed to blur, making it difficult to focus. The evening's shadows crept across the pavement, enveloping her in a ghostly embrace.

Alone and with no one to offer solace, she felt her strength wane. Why now? Why, when all she needed was a moment of respite?

The once-lively detective struggled to catch her breath, pressing her hand to the wound in her side, her pain feeling the jagged edges of glass piercing her skin. Despite her best efforts, her legs buckled beneath her, causing her to collapse onto the unforgiving concrete.

She fumbled for her phone. Her fingers trembled as she played an old voicemail.

"Reece, I found this amazing place for our weekend getaway. Trust me, it's perfect. Just us, a cozy cabin, and the wilderness. Can't wait to get away from it all. Love you."

As his sweet voice rang out like music, the vibrant colors of her life seemed to fade, leaving her in a monochromatic world devoid of light. She choked back a bitter laugh. Get away from it all? Wasn't she doing that now, in the worst possible way?

The cold fingers of fate gripped her, and she could feel herself slipping away, her consciousness flickering like a dying flame, the approaching darkness threatening to swallow her whole.

Her eyes fluttered as she lay there. The cold seeped into her bones, her life-force draining as the pool of blood grew larger beneath her.

"I'm sorry," she murmured. Her breaths now came in shallow gasps, the shadows of her past swirling around her, a cacophony of memories and regrets.

Sirens wailed in the distance as her vision blurred. Reece gritted her teeth. The wound in her side burned with agony, the pain reminding her of her mortality.

Her thoughts whirled, spinning like a dervish, each one a new facet of the anguish she felt. Memories, regrets, and unspoken words, they all haunted her as she clung to the edge.

Is this it? Is this where it all ends?

The monsoon rain had just ended, and the droplets of water clinging to the nearby cacti glistened like a thousand tiny diamonds. Her fingertips grazed the damp brick wall she lay by. Its rough texture absorbed the slickness of her bloodied hands.

She tried to remember the warmth of the Arizona sun on her face, the smell of fresh tortillas from a nearby street vendor, and the laughter of her friends, but they all seemed so far away now.

As she began to lose herself to the darkness, the sirens grew louder, their shrill cry seeming like a cruel joke, like hope snatched away just as it was within reach.

In the background, the voicemail played again, his voice a reminder of what she'd lost.

Her eyes shut. Her grip on reality faltered. The sound of the sirens seemed to exist at the end of a very long tunnel, falling farther and farther away.

And then…silence.

1

DECADES EARLIER

THE SCENT OF FRESHLY BAKED COOKIES filled the home. Sunlight bathed the living room, adding to the warmth of the weekend morning.

Little Reece Cannon savored each chocolate-chip bite, reveling in the tender embrace of her father Sandy's arms as he wrapped his arms around her. Laughter echoed through the kitchen.

At eight years old, Reece was the epitome of innocence and joy, her days spent exploring and making memories.

"Ready for an adventure, kiddo?" Sandy asked, his eyes twinkling with mischief.

Reece immediately jumped up and stuffed the rest of the cookie in her mouth, the thrill of the unknown making her wiggle and jump and do a happy dance like kids do.

"Where are we going, Dad?"

Sandy flashed her a knowing smile. "To visit Genie Thompson. Remember how she went away on vacation? She just got back, and she called up mom to say she brought you a little something, a souvenir."

Reece's eyes lit up with excitement, the allure of a foreign treasure too enticing to resist. In moments, they were out the door, the world a brilliant canvas of possibilities stretching out before them.

Ms. Thompson had lived down the street for years—a no-nonsense woman feared by most of the neighborhood kids.

"She's rough around the edges, but she's had a rough life," Sandy explained, his tone contemplative. "People like her—they just need a little compassion, Reece. It can make all the difference, no?"

Reece smiled, nodding, not really understanding what he meant. Or really caring.

As they drove, Reece chattered incessantly about school, friends, and the upcoming summer vacation. Sandy listened intently, offering words of encouragement and wisdom.

But when they finally arrived, a heavy silence enveloped the residence. It was an unassuming house with landscaping rocks and manicured bushes. But something seemed off. The door stood slightly ajar.

Reece remembered Ms. Thompson once explaining the benefits of sunlight while tending to the plethora of potted plants in her home—but the curtains were currently drawn even though it was late morning.

Her dad seemed to hesitate, concern written on his face. "Reece, wait in the car," he instructed, his voice firm. "I need to check something out."

Reece sensed her father's unease. She watched as he approached the house, curiosity gnawing at her insides. She couldn't shake the feeling that something was wrong. Her instincts screamed at her to follow.

And so, she did.

Slipping out of the car, she crept towards the front door, her childlike wonder getting the better of her. As she drew closer, the silence seemed to intensify, and a shiver of apprehension trickled through Reece.

She stepped through the entrance. Her breath instantly caught in her throat. The living room was in shambles, furniture overturned and shattered glass lay scattered across the floor. Fear crept in then, a cold, suffocating grip. She'd never seen anything like this before.

She watched her father proceed through the wreckage seemingly unaware of her presence. Though Reece should have remained beyond the doorway, the urge to know the truth of this situation was too strong. Following in his footsteps, she stepped into the chaos, her small frame making no noise on the carpet.

Then she saw her.

Reece was no stranger to scraped knees or the occasional playground injury, but this was a level of brutality she'd never imagined possible. The sheer horror of the sight made her knees buckle. Her legs threatened to give out.

Her father knelt by Ms. Thompson's side, grasping her wrist in search of a pulse. In a hushed tone, he uttered her name, "Genie?"

There, in the center of the kitchen, lay the broken body of Ms. Thompson. Her lifeless eyes stared up at the ceiling, the light within them snuffed out. She lay sprawled, her once pristine white blouse stained crimson.

Reece had never seen death up close. Nor had she ever experienced the raw, unfiltered atrocity of something like this.

She stood there transfixed, rooted to the spot, her eyes wide with terror. The world seemed to slow down, each second stretching into an eternity as she tried to comprehend the scene before her.

The room began to spin, the walls closing in as Reece struggled to breathe.

Her terrified cry shattered the stillness. Sandy turned and raced towards Reece, who was still screaming, her eyes locked on the horrific sight. Her father acted quickly, picking her up and rushing her back to the open air outside.

Yet the nightmare persisted.

Her father's voice was a distant echo, barely registering in her mind as he tried to console her.

As the police arrived, the house erupted into a flurry of activity. Officers swarmed, and questions flew like gunfire, each one a bullet aimed at the heart of Reece's shattered innocence. She struggled to answer, her mind reeling from the trauma of what she'd witnessed.

Reece's world crumbled that day, the veneer of invincible-like safety ripped away in an instant. She watched her father speak with the officers, his visage stoic.

As the hours dragged on, the grim reality of her new world settled in. It had become a darker place, a shadowy realm where monsters lurked around every corner.

She clung to her father ceaselessly, her small frame trembling with fear and exhaustion.

The sun had long since set, the once warm and inviting day supplanted by a terrifying nocturnal cloak. Her father held her close as she lay wakeful, hours beyond her bedtime, his eyes filled with a mixture of love and helplessness. Though she lacked the words, she intuited his thoughts—that he'd failed to protect his daughter from the horrors of the world.

As sleep finally claimed her that night, a single question hung in the air.

Who could have done this?

And in the pit of her stomach, a nascent dread took root within her, growing with each passing moment.

Who would be next?

Who is Reece Cannon?

From the first intriguing pages of *Blatant Lies* to the heart-stopping finale of *Crescent*, the Reece Cannon series offers readers a journey of true transformation rarely seen in modern thriller literature.

This isn't your typical series where the main character remains static.

Reece is not confined within the traditional boundaries of the genre; instead, she shatters them, forging a path that is unique to her.

Reece begins her journey as a rookie deputy for the Pima County Sheriff's Department. She's eager for excitement, thirsty for justice, and above all, naïve. This book sees the first major change in Reece, pushing her from a greenhorn cop to a seasoned detective, stepping up from a rookie to a game-changer.

In *Mind of a Killer*, we see Reece not just investigating crimes, but dissecting the mind of a cold-blooded predator. The growing body count, the heart-wrenching secrets within her own family, and a personal target on her back, all contribute to a significant evolution in her character, making her a more discerning and relentless detective.

By *If You Hurt Her*, Reece transitions from the observer to the participant, her trajectory from being on the outside looking in, to being thrust within the abyss of crime and corruption.

In *Hidden and Watching*, Reece's world spirals out of control. Investigating a powerful crime syndicate, she stumbles upon evidence that threatens to expose the international criminal organization's illicit activities— while also finding out it's connected to her own family.

This discovery brings with it an unprecedented level of danger, and for the first time, Reece experiences the chilling fear and helplessness of becoming an abductee.

Her abduction, far from breaking her, instead becomes the crucible in which her character is further forged. It deepens her resolve and sparks a fire within her. But it's not just a matter of will. She recognizes that she must become stronger, sharper, and more lethal if she's to prevail.

In book 6, *Her Perfect Grave*, Reece leaves the sheriff's department, no longer a detective. She goes on a personal journey to take down the crime syndicate her family is a part of, once and for all.

She takes charge of her own destiny, yet her connection with the criminal underworld deepens. This dramatic shift in her career trajectory, coupled with her battles against personal demons, sees her becoming a well-rounded, complex character with a wealth of experience and a burdensome load of regrets and resentments.

As Reece steps into the mysterious agency Sub Rosa in *Try to Breathe*, her past experiences have molded her into a skilled and cunning special agent. She's done the physical and mental training. Her combat skills have been honed, and she's now mastered the ability to protect herself and others in hostile situations.

In *Betrayal and Justice*, Reece Cannon's journey progresses, subtly shifting from an individual's quest against crime to a broader indictment of the very institutions that are supposed to uphold the law and maintain order. It's not the criminals who threaten her most now; it's those she once trusted implicitly.

Her interactions with authority, once marked by respect and obedience, now bristle with skepticism and defiance. She realizes that not all villains lurk in the shadows of the criminal underworld; some wear the mantle of authority and hide in plain sight.

But it's not just about uncovering the corruption; it's about grappling with the betrayal of her colleagues, her superiors, and the very system she pledged to serve. The battle scars she wears aren't just from physical combat anymore; they are the wounds of profound personal and professional betrayal.

By *Song of Ruse*, Reece Cannon's narrative acquires an enigmatic, yet intriguing twist. She finds herself in uncharted territories of her mind, the compass of her memory spinning aimlessly, lost in a haze of amnesia. The bonds that tethered her to her past, to her sense of self, have come undone.

Reece is a woman unbound by rules and unsullied by affiliations. She treads the gray areas of morality, sidestepping her conventional sense of right and wrong to partner with characters that were once silhouettes on the other side of the law.

The dance with ambiguity continues in the final installment, *Crescent*. Reece is no longer bound by any loyalties, rules, or institutions. She has evolved into a woman who walks a solitary path, dictated by her personal quest and fueled by a need for answers, regardless of the chaotic echoes that follow her.

The repercussions of her actions send ripples through her circles, leaving those who once knew her reeling, struggling to comprehend her transformation.

This change in Reece is alarming to some, inspiring to others, and unnerving to most. The once-law-abiding detective now blurs the lines, bending rules and breaking conventions.

Yet, even in this state of turmoil, Reece's character shines with an unyielding tenacity. Her resilience is the silver lining in her stormy journey, and her defiance, the constant North Star guiding her through the tumultuous seas of uncertainty. No matter the stakes, the chaos, or the pain, Reece stays true to herself. She remains Reece Cannon—a force to reckon with, a woman of her own making.

Crescent wraps up this saga with Reece as an enigma that challenges the conventional hero's archetype. The narrative cements her status as a fiercely independent character, steadfast in her pursuit of truth and justice, no matter how blurry the lines between right and wrong might appear.

The *Reece Cannon Thriller* series is a testament to the power of transformation and the human capacity to adapt and evolve. It's a rollercoaster ride of emotions, an intricate tapestry of interpersonal dynamics, a deep dive into the human psyche, and above all, an extraordinary character journey that keeps readers engaged from start to finish.

Readers are thus left with a narrative that encourages them to question their own understanding of heroes and antiheroes, righteousness and rebellion. It pushes them to acknowledge that strength comes in many forms and that it is often born of struggle and resilience. The Reece Cannon series, as a whole, is an exquisite exploration of the human condition and a tribute to the endurance of the spirit, leaving a resounding impact that lingers well beyond the final page.

The series is a must-read for those who appreciate a layered, complex, and dynamic protagonist who defies the conventions of the genre.

Author Note

If you've read this far, I want to sincerely say THANK YOU for beginning this journey with Reece Cannon.

We couldn't do it without you.

One huge thing that you can do for Reece is to leave a quick review. It only takes a second, but she will be extremely grateful.

Even just a few words can make a difference for an author like Paul Knox.

Cheers,
Paul

Titles listed in order
A Reece Cannon Thriller

Made in United States
North Haven, CT
24 August 2024

56510592R00124